THE THIRD DRAGON

Unknown to all three of the teenagers, a man had been watching John and Jenny climb up the third dragon to the cave, and saw them come down again. When they had gone their different ways, he too took the path up the hill. As he came to the cave, he paused, then carefully drew out a revolver. Taking a firm grip of the weapon, he advanced towards the place where Xu was sitting, quietly humming to himself.

Other titles in the Mystery Thriller series include:

THE THIRD DRAGON

by
GARRY KILWORTH
Illustrated by Mel Bramich

Hippo Books
Scholastic Publications Limited
London

Scholastic Publications Ltd.,
10 Earlham Street, London WC2H 9RX, UK

Scholastic Inc.,
730 Broadway, New York, NY 10003, USA

Scholastic Canada Ltd.,
123 Newkirk Road, Richmond Hill,
Ontario L4C 3G5, Canada

Ashton Scholastic Pty Ltd.,
P O Box 579, Gosford, New South Wales,
Australia

Ashton Scholastic Ltd.,
Private Bag 1, Penrose, Auckland,
New Zealand

First published 1991

Text copyright © Garry Kilworth, 1991
Illustration copyright © Mel Bramich, 1991

ISBN 0 590 76416 0

Typeset by AKM Associates (UK) Ltd., Southall, London
Printed by Cox and Wyman Ltd., Reading, Berks

To Daniel Moseley

Chapter One

Xu had been one of the students in Tiananmen Square when the Chinese army had first begun firing their weapons into the demonstrators. Two of Xu's friends fell near his feet and Xu began running, into the darkness, to escape the mayhem. Jumping over bicycles crushed by the tanks of the People's Liberation Army, he ran down a side street, his heart pounding in his chest. He had never believed that the PLA would shoot the students, not for a minute. The PLA represented the people, they weren't supposed ever to be used *against* them.

Xu found a bicycle and began pedalling away from the scene of horror that was behind him in Tiananmen Square. He could still hear the shooting and the screams. People were coming out of their houses now to witness the carnage – they too were being attacked by the soldiers. Xu knew that some of the students had vowed not to leave the Square until the reforms they had requested were accepted by the government.

He guessed that most of his comrades would die.

Xu met up with two more students and they made their way south, towards Hong Kong. The leaders of the "revolution", such as Wuerkaixi, would be hunted down first. Xu and his two comrades, one a girl, would only be caught if they were stopped and questioned outside Beijing. Their names were not yet known to the authorities.

They managed to stow away in a railway car amongst pigs bound for the province of Guangdong, which bordered the British Crown Colony of Hong Kong. They were on the train for five days, without food, though they had some water between them. They ate the mash which was pushed through the bottom slats of the car for the pigs to eat. The pigs resented their presence and Xu was bitten twice by a sow from whose trough he tried to steal mash.

Two days after that, Xu managed to get in contact with a Hong Kong triad gang, smugglers who also specialised in transporting illegal immigrants from Guangdong to Hong Kong in high-speed launches, propelled by a triple set of powerful engines.

But Xu had no money and was rejected.

Undaunted, he and his two companions decided to swim across the stretch of sea which separated

Guangdong from the New Territories of Hong Kong. They planned to do the swim at night, because they had been told by local people that the British Gurkhas patrolled the border and would be less likely to catch them in the darkness. Creeping through the village of Sha Tau Kok, they entered the waters of Starling Inlet, and began their dangerous journey.

The other male student was not a good swimmer and had to turn back after a few hundred yards. The girl stayed with him, but unfortunately the inlet was used for the dumping of fish waste and there were predatory fish in these waters. He did not even see his companion go, but heard a flurry nearby, and the fear in her cry was unmistakable. When he reached the far shore, exhausted, and pulled himself out of the sea, she was nowhere to be seen. Xu guessed that perhaps a lone shark had taken her, and for the first time since that night in Tiananmen Square, he began to cry.

Once he had recovered his composure, Xu made his way down into the New Territories, hoping to find someone to help him. His difficulty was that he was a Han Chinese, and spoke only Mandarin dialect, while most Hong Kong Chinese spoke Cantonese. Although the Chinese written characters are understandable by all the people of China, their spoken languages are quite different. Xu would have to draw the characters on his palm, with his forefinger, if he wanted to be understood by a Cantonese speaker. This was a common way of communicating between two speakers of different dialects. However, the first few people he came across were Hakka women, doing repair work on the roads early in the morning, and they were too busy to pay attention to him. They shook their heads in impatience, the black frills of their tribal hats flicking this way and that as they did so.

Xu walked on, hoping to find someone sympathetic enough to listen to his cry for help.

Chapter Two

Happy Valley Stadium on Hong Kong Island was a sea of dark-haired people dressed in the traditional Chinese mourning colours of white and black. It was the 12th of June, 1989, and just a few days previously in Tiananmen Square, Beijing, the capital of mainland China, hundreds, perhaps thousands of students, had been massacred by the PLA.

The people sitting quietly on the Happy Valley racecourse, many openly weeping, were there to pay their respects to the dead students of mainland China. It was an awesome sight – almost a million Hong Kong citizens – and one John Tenniel would never forget. Some of the faces wore stunned or bewildered expressions, as if they could not believe the massacre had actually happened. Others looked angry, or sad, or depressed. There were many tears. Occasionally they cried with their faces buried in their hands, for privacy.

John was only quarter Chinese himself. His father was English and his mother half-Cantonese, half-Portugese. John's parents had met in the Portugese colony of Macau, on the other side of the Pearl River from Hong Kong, had fallen in love and married. Perhaps in most places in the world, people would have thought John had rather exotic parents, but in Hong Kong mixed marriages were common.

Sitting on either side of John, on the Happy Valley turf, were his two best friends.

Jenny Lee, on his left, was a Hong Kong born Chinese girl with a quick mind and an irrepressible sense of fun. Jenny's mother had come down from Canton when she was seventeen, and met and married her father, a local businessman.

Peter Patterson, on his right, was an expatriate family's child, originally from Britain. Peter's parents had lived in Hong Kong for twenty-three years. Mr Patterson was terribly proud of the city he had seen blossom into one of the busiest harbours in the world. The words "Hong Kong" mean "Fragrant Harbour", from the time the port was full of ships bearing spices.

The three friends were all the same age. They attended the same classes at the King Edward High School on Waterloo Road, and went to the same church on Sundays.

A man stood up from amongst the vast crowd, holding a piece of paper in his hand. He began leading a chant, which gradually swelled in volume throughout the stadium, until a million voices were replying to his questions.

"Who has died for democracy?" he cried.

"The students in Tiananmen Square!" came the deafening reply.

Some of the policemen, there to keep the demonstration under control, began to look a little nervous. The authorities had not expected so many people. However, there had been no trouble during any of the demonstrations so far, and it did not look as if there was going to be any this time.

"We'd better be getting home, I suppose," said John, and both Jenny and Peter nodded.

"It's almost four," said Jenny. "My parents will get worried if I stay out too long. You know what they're like."

A little disappointed that they could not stay for the march to the Bank of China building, where a further demonstration was to take place, the three companions picked up their lunch boxes and stepped carefully through the masses of silent people, nodding to a few friends and acquaintances as they did so.

They made their way from Happy Valley to the Star Ferry, to cross the harbour. On the other side they would catch the MTR underground train to Kowloon Tong, where they lived.

The colony of Hong Kong was split into three

parts: Hong Kong Island, Kowloon, and the New Territories. The Island and Kowloon peninsula were both crammed with high rise buildings and skyscrapers, narrow streets, and blocks of tenement flats.

The New Territories, though its villages had grown upwards to become tight little skyscraper towns, was mostly hills, inlets and country parks. Separating the Kowloon from the New Territories was a range of hills known as the Nine Dragons.

To the Chinese, every hill and mountain is a dragon.

John's block of flats was near to the Third Dragon.

Although they did not know it, they were being followed from the stadium by a round-faced man, the pupils of whose eyes were like insects. He kept pace with them, just a few feet behind, as they came to the Star Ferry and boarded the boat for the short trip across the harbour.

He lit a cigarette and flicked the match over the rail into the water. It sizzled as it hit the surface. Then he moved close enough to the three friends to hear what they were saying, but kept his back to them. From his pocket he took out a small notebook and began to record their conversation.

John was saying, "Are you two doing anything this evening?"

Peter replied, "Nah. Still got some maths to do."

"What about you, Jenny?" asked John.

"Same as Peter," she replied. "Homework."

The little round-faced man took out a notebook

and wrote 'JENNY' and 'PETER'. He stayed there the whole journey, taking down snippets of information, such as where they were going, who their friends were, the name of their school. When they reached the other side, he left the boat just ahead of them, and cleverly stayed there, as if he were only going the same way as they were by accident.

There was a big cardboard notice outside Star Ferry Terminal on the Kowloon side, which read:
HEY HEY PLA, HOW MANY KIDS DID YOU KILL TODAY?
The student protest in China had turned into a terrible tragedy and emotions were running high in Hong Kong. In 1997 the British were going to hand back the whole colony of Hong Kong, which they had ruled for over a hundred years, to the Government of China. Feelings about what would happen to Hong Kong after 1997 had turned from anxiousness to terror. The soldiers of the PLA that had shot the students, would be marching through the streets of Kowloon, Central, Wanchai, Stanley, Tsimshatsui, and all the other districts of Hong Kong, and no one knew what was going to happen after that. The people of Hong Kong were used to many freedoms that were not given to the rest of their race in mainland China, and they were afraid they would lose them all overnight.

When they reached Kowloon Tong station, and alighted from their train, the three friends had a short conference.

"School tomorrow," said Peter, making a face.

"Geography," groaned Jenny. She always moaned along with Peter, because she knew he disliked school, preferring sports and games and open-air activities. Secretly, however, Jenny loved school and was a very bright student.

"I suppose I'll have to get some homework done tonight." Like most Chinese students, she was highly competitive, her family placing success in education above all things.

"Don't forget we're playing football tomorrow," said Peter to John.

Inwardly, John groaned at this news. He was much better at individual sports, and hated team games. His team mates always shouted at him because he seemed to have a knack of being in the wrong place most of the time.

"I won't forget," he said. "Got to go now. Bye Jenny, bye Pete. See you at eight."

"Right," replied the other two, almost in chorus.

John climbed aboard a bus and put one and a half dollars in the slot by the door. When he looked down through the window, he could see a round-faced man with funny eyes writing the number of the bus down in a notebook. John thought he had seen the man before, but shrugged it off.

A few moments later the bus pulled out and began climbing a hill to reach John's block of flats. They lived in a building called Vista Panorama which his mother insisted on calling Vista Paranoia, because the occupants barricaded themselves inside layers of double and triple glazed windows to escape the external noise.

His father was home, trying to read a handful of newspaper clippings. He looked extremely cross. Mr Tenniel worked for a company called China Light and Power which supplied electricity to Kowloon. He was an engineer.

John's mother was a teacher at Beacon Hill Primary School. She was cutting things up on the living-room table. She seemed to cut things up most weekends: magazines, pictures, newspapers. With the cuttings she formed mysterious heaps in corners of the flat. The room looked as if a very neat whirlwind had passed through it. John's father sometimes didn't manage to reach his Sunday paper before his wife's scissors had somehow flown across the living-room and snipped it into squares, oblongs and L-shaped geometrical figures. He used to complain bitterly whenever this happened.

"Can't even read my own newspaper," he said, as John walked through the door. "I mean it's not much to ask, is it? You can have the thing once I've read it, but I hate sorting through heaps of litter for half an article I really wanted to read."

He held up a tiny square of paper for John to witness. Mum always had some scheme on the go and while she was in the middle of such things the rest of the family had to grin and bear the disruption to the household.

"Sorry dear," replied his mother. "I don't under-stand how it happened. I wasn't even working on that

11

side of the room. Are you sure you didn't give it to me yourself?"

"Of course I'm sure. What are you doing with all those cuttings anyway?" he asked in an exasperated tone. "What on earth are you doing with them?"

"Oh, you know," said Mrs Tenniel. "I get the children to make collages for one thing. Pieces of paper are always useful when you've got a class full of infants and a rainy day outside."

"How about teaching them times tables and all those things *I* had to learn at school."

She laughed and shook her head at this.

"We don't teach things by rote any more. That's about as fashionable as bell-bottom trousers."

"Careful Mum," said John, "they're coming back in."

"Well, luminous socks then," she turned her attention to her son. "How was the rally dear? We saw some of it on TV. I was a bit worried. I didn't expect there to be so many people . . ."

"Oh, it was all right. I mean, it *wasn't* all right, but we were safe enough. I told you we would be."

His father shook his head.

"That's not the point, John. Those rallies are getting too big. I know they've been peaceful up until now, but it only needs one person to panic. We all feel strongly about the shooting of those students up in China, but I think the protest has been made. We don't want you to go to any more."

John felt the usual frustration that built up in his chest when his parents began to assert their authority.

"Aw, Dad . . ."

"No, never mind 'aw Dad' – you've been on three of those rallies. That's enough. No arguments. I think we've been far too irresponsible as parents as it is."

"But Jenny and Peter . . ."

John's mother spoke now.

"Their parents feel the same way as we do, John."

John cried, "You've been plotting!"

Mr Tenniel nodded, emphatically.

"If that's what you want to call it, fair enough. Parents are entitled to plot against their kids when it's for their own good. Now, I said no arguments, and I meant it. Let's call it a day, okay?"

John nodded. He knew his parents and once they dug their heels in there was no moving them.

He went and had a cold shower, since the temperatures were around 30 centigrade, changed into fresh shorts and T-shirt, and rejoined his parents in the living-room. Their minor battle concerning the newspaper was over and his mother was lovingly gathering up her clippings to add them to the stacks already in the spare room.

"Can I help you with those?" he asked.

"No thank you dear, I can manage."

"You can help me cook the dinner," said his father, rising from his rattan chair. "Stir fry. Needs a lot of preparation."

"Aw, Dad. You know how fussy you are about how to cut up aubergines and things. I never get it right for you. Mum's pretty handy at cutting things up."

13

His father crooked a finger.

"You and me, son. It's our turn. Right, now you do the chillis . . ."

"They make my eyes water."

". . . and do them *properly*. Cutting up vegetables is an art form. Most British people just get a knife and hack a carrot or onion to pieces. Long strips, like little orange fish. Beautiful. And the onion in half-rings . . ." And so he went on, while John did his best to cut the chillis into thread-like pieces, at the same time keeping his fingers away from his eyes, before he had washed them thoroughly.

That evening, after dinner, they watched the news on the English spoken Pearl channel of Hong Kong television. The main news was of course the demonstrations and the continuing events in China. The newscaster announced that China was rounding up dissidents and executions were taking place. Nevertheless, some of the students from Tiananmen Square were making their way to the borders and crossing over into sanctuary. None had yet arrived in Hong Kong, however, and it was suggested that if they did the issue would be a very sensitive one. Hong Kong was going to be handed back to China in 1997, only eight years from the date of the massacre, and offering political asylum to China's dissidents would be seen by the Chinese government as a subversive act. They were still in the process of negotiating terms of agreement for the handover, and the British Governor of the Crown Colony, Sir David Wilson, would not want to jeopardise the future of the Hong

Kong Chinese by making those talks impossible.

"I don't understand what they mean by that," said John's younger brother, Alex, after the programme was over. "I think old Willy should tell China to take a running jump over the Great Wall."

Alex was ten years old and full of juvenile passion over any injustice in the world.

"Trouble is, there's this business about *face*," John said, having witnessed this cultural aspect of Chinese pride many times. "If the Chinese government think it's going to lose face, it'll just be obstructive in the talks."

John had only that Friday encountered the problem of face. He had entered a music shop and asked if they had a cassette tape of the Australian rock group Midnight Oil's *Diesel and Dust*. The shop assistant, a young Chinese, nodded and said yes. He disappeared into the back of the shop, leaving John waiting.

John assumed the young man was looking for the tape in his stock, but in fact he never reappeared and John then realised he did *not* have *Diesel and Dust* but would have lost face by saying so. Eventually John knew the young man would not return until John had left the shop, which he did immediately.

On the other hand, there were plenty of myths about oriental people which were false. It was not true, for instance, that the Chinese were inscrutable. The morning after the massacre, the Hong Kong Chinese had been out in the streets, openly weeping. Caught up in the emotional atmosphere, John had cried too. Parents in China are permitted only one child for each family. Every one of those young men and women killed in the massacre would leave a family childless. A whole generation wiped out in one night.

"I don't care about *obstructive*," said Alex. "If I was a student I'd just bash their *face* in, ha, ha."

"Is that supposed to be a joke," said John, wearily.

"Not supposed to be, it flippin' well is a joke," cried Alex in glee.

"Never mind the jokes, eat the dinner," said their father.

Alex scowled, his expression going from smug to sour in a second. John gave up on him. There was only two years between them, but it might as well have been a hundred. They had absolutely nothing in common and only used each other for company when there was no one else around.

After dinner John had homework to do. Like his pals he always left his until the last minute, despite promises to do it before the weekend. Alex threatened to go into the spare room and make paper aeroplanes out of his mother's scraps, but everyone knew he was just trying it on, so they ignored him. Alex liked attention and was always saying something out-rageous, like, "I think I'll become a terrorist when I grow up." His parents were horrified by him – or at least pretended to be – while John merely shook his head and sighed.

Brothers were just things you had to put up with because your parents refused to get rid of them, even when they turned out like Alex.

"Can't we just sneak back to Hong Kong without him?" John had said once, while they were having breakfast on holiday in Malaysia.

"Can't be done," his father sighed. "We're stuck with him and that's that."

"Ha, ha!" cried Alex, clamping a treacled hand on his brother's arm. "Stuck with me, and that's that!"

Chapter Three

There was seldom a time in the middle of the night when John could not hear the sound of traffic outside his bedroom window. The cars and trucks, buses and vans, roared their way through to the early hours, paused for a perhaps an hour, then rose again like rested dragons to roar into the day and beyond. An early bird, using John's bedroom air conditioner as a perch, battled with its song against the waves of noise. It was this sound, to which John was unused, that woke him from his sleep.

He stumbled to the bathroom and showered and cleaned his teeth before his brother awoke and added his own brand of noise pollution to the atmosphere of Hong Kong. Then he dressed and gathered together the books he would need at school that day. At the last moment he remembered that the class was going to Mai Po Marshes, the bird sanctuary in the extreme north of the New Territories, right on the border of China. He packed the 7 x 21 binoculars his father had given him for his birthday.

John managed to get out of the house before Alex emerged with his early morning "jokes" and made his way to school. He could have taken the bus, but since he had plenty of time he walked.

As he strolled through the small park there were dozens of Chinese people doing their tai chi exercises on the grass, drawing dragons and lions and snakes with their body movements. He stood and watched them for a moment. His mother, being half-Chinese, had been raised in the belief that daily tai chi was good for both the spirit and the body.

He left the fitness fanatics to their artistic limb and body poses, and walked on, past the elderly Chinese out walking with their caged birds. Sometimes they hung them in the trees so that the tame bird could learn songs from the wild birds.

Once, John had the prickly sensation that he was being followed down a long alley and turned quickly to see if it was true. Flame trees from gardens abutting the alley extended feathery-leaved branches over the alley walls, keeping it permanently in the shade. The light was poor and eerie which, along with the unusual silence, worried him.

The long straight passage was almost empty, however, except for a cat amongst some bags of rubbish, but the feeling of having his footsteps dogged refused to leave him.

When he reached the road at the far end, there were people hurrying towards the MTR station, which was close to the school. John heaved a little sigh of relief, at the same time telling himself that he was being stupid. It was only a *feeling*, after all.

He was glad when he finally reached the school gates. Once he was inside the school, all threatening thoughts fell from him and more practical worries took over, like how his homework was going to be received by Slimeball, his form teacher.

At three o'clock there was a game of football. John was supposed to be a sweeper, but the day was damp and hot, and he was glad when the match was stopped because a cobra had been seen in the tall verge grass.

When he had changed back into his school shirt and shorts, the coach arrived to take the class to Mai Po Marshes.

"Did you remember your bins?" asked Peter, as they climbed abroad.

John nodded, showing him the binoculars.

"Forgot mine," said Peter, sourly.

Jenny said, "Never mind. They often have spare pairs to hand out. Hopefully most people have brought some. If not you can share mine."

The coach pulled out at four o'clock and drove straight into the mass of traffic waiting to go through the Lion Rock tunnel which passed through the range of mountains separating Kowloon from the New Territories. Mr Ball – or Slimeball as he was affectionately known amongst his students – explained what they were going to do.

"Mai Pao was founded by Peter Scott, the naturalist – bit before your time, I expect. Anyway, it's one of the stop-over places for birds migrating south from Russia and northern China, to the tropics and Australasia. Birds, like aircraft on long-haul flights, need places to refuel and rest, before continuing their journey. Being marshland, there are of course a lot of waders and water birds, so try and spot as many as you can, such as the rare spoonbilled sandpiper or the red-necked stint . . ."

"Sir?" said Jameson Master, a youth with a permanently peeling nose. "Sir, will there be any white-bellied sea eagles swooping out of the blue like kamikaze planes, their hooked beaks and talons sharpened to razor keenness, and ripping the other birds to bits, showering blood all over the place and leaving intestines dangling from the branches of trees . . ."

Slimeball sighed the sigh of a long-suffering teacher.

"JM, take a hundred lines."

"Yes, sir, it was worth it, sir."

The coach passed by the Marine Police Station on the Tolo Highway, where high-speed launches were stacked in the yard, their triple engines wrapped about with chains. These were boats that had been confiscated from smugglers caught in and around Hong Kong.

They reached Mai Po Marshes and were met by a small young Chinese man who told them in English that he was their guide for the next two hours. Much to Peter's delight, he issued binoculars to all those without them, and the group proceeded to the first hide, out on the edge of the marshes and hidden by clumps of feathery-leaved bamboo.

The class spent two hours in the hide, watching and being lectured by Slimeball on why each individual bird was important to the planet earth.

"We are all part of the jigsaw, and when a piece goes missing, the jigsaw loses some of its worth. If too many pieces go missing, it becomes a useless item, fit only for the rubbish bin. Of course this doesn't include the piece of jigsaw we call JM, without whom the world would be a better place . . ."

"Bloomin' cheek," muttered Jameson Master, "I don't have to take this. My dad pays his taxes . . ."

Suddenly there was the sound of distant shouting, and shrill whistles blowing. The commotion seemed to be coming from the fringe of Mai Po marshes, by the border with China.

John put his binoculars to his eyes.

At first he could see nothing but waving grass, and bamboo, but then he caught a glimpse of someone running, desperately trying to lose some pursuers. It was a man in ragged shorts and T-shirt and he was trying to outrun some soldiers.

"What's happening?" said Peter.

"Look's like someone's climbed over the border

fence," replied John, still peering intently through his binoculars.

"Who's chasing him? The Chinese?"

"No, I think it's the Gurkhas," answered John.

Sure enough he could see the Nepalese soldiers who guarded the border chasing the man across the marshes. It looked difficult terrain to cross, being boggy, and the Chinese man was having a hard time keeping his feet. John could see the agony in the young man's face, his chest heaving with laboured breathing, the leadenness in his legs. No doubt he had been running for some time, to get across no-man's land, and had probably been hoping that there would be no Gurkhas to pass once he reached the Hong Kong fence. Unluckily for him, a patrol must have been going by at that time. In any case, there were lookout posts along the frontier, just watching for people like him.

"Come on," whispered Jenny, looking through her own binoculars, "you can make it."

Gradually, all the class began muttering, then calling out loud, and finally they were cheering the man on, hoping he would outrun the border guards. After all, he was not a criminal. He was just someone who had heard that there was a better life to be had beyond the wire, in Hong Kong, and he had decided to risk it.

"Quiet!" ordered Mr Ball.

The children fell dutifully silent. They knew from the tone of his voice that Slimeball really meant it.

Still, they were not told to stop watching, and it

23

was doubtful they would have obeyed if Slimeball had gone that far. The whole incident had them spellbound.

At one point, it seemed as if the runner was putting distance between himself and his pursuers. He was almost up to the hide now and John had lowered his binoculars to stare directly down on the runner. The man stopped, looked up at the row of children in the hide. His expression was full of despair. John could see the pleading in his eyes, but there was nothing anyone could do to help him. He would be caught and sent back to China, just as dozens of his countrymen were every day.

When he tried to run again, the man's feet stuck in the bog. The more he struggled, the deeper went his legs, until he was up to his knees in black sludge. Eventually, the soldiers arrived, put a plank out onto the marsh, and pulled the man free. He was led away with his head hanging down. He had lost face in front of the children. His dignity had been hurt when he was wallowing in the mud and he did not want anyone to see his eyes. He was really only a youth, his legs caked in foul-smelling mud, and John felt terribly sorry for him.

"Nearly made it," said Peter.

"No, they would have caught him," said John. "Even if he had made the hard ground, where could he have run to from here? There's nowhere to hide around here, is there?"

"Still," said Jenny, "he would have given them a run for their money, if he'd got past us, wouldn't he?"

24

"Right," shouted Slimeball, "that's enough chatter all of you. Excitement's over. Let's get back to work. Now can anyone tell me the name of that bird over there?"

At six-thirty they boarded the coach again and drove south, heading back to the Lion Rock tunnel. Some of the students, weary after trudging over the marshes, fell asleep. Peter dozed and Jenny went off into a reverie. John stared out of the windows, watching the dusk sweeping in over the waters of the Tolo Harbour. The darkness came in fast, like a giant fruit bat, to fold its wings over the landscape. Up on Monkey Mountain, above the flats where John lived, the wild monkeys would be settling for the night.

When he arrived home the flat was in darkness and John remembered that his parents had gone to see a play at the new cultural centre. Alex was staying over with a neighbourhood friend. John opened the door with his own key and threw his school stuff in an armchair, before going to the kitchen to get a drink from the fridge.

When he switched on the kitchen light, he got the fright of his life. Standing by the fridge, eating some cold rice, was a Chinese boy not much older than himself. He was ragged and dirty, and his feet were bleeding through his thin shoes.

Both boys stared at each other with shocked expressions, and neither of them said anything or moved for at least two minutes. John wondered whether to run, shout for help, or tackle the youth on

25

his own. However, something about the other boy's appearance made him hold back from all three actions. Although the youth was taller than John, he was much thinner. He appeared to be exhausted, and indeed looked weak from starvation. This was no ordinary burglar. He had not turned the place upside-down looking for money, but had made straight for the smell of food. It was sheer hunger that had driven him to enter the flat, that much was obvious.

Finally, John spoke. "How did you get in here?" he said in Cantonese.

The youth swallowed a mouthful of rice, then rattled off something in a dialect John did not understand. It sounded like none of the dialects John had heard before: not Hakkanese, Shanghaiese or Hokkien, nor even his own second language, Cantonese.

"*Nei gwong dong wae – aa?*," John said, asking if the other spoke Cantonese.

There was no response. Just a wide-eyed stare. John wondered if he were getting his 'tones' right, for Cantonese is a sing-song language and the same word can mean many things. It is the tone in which the word is said which provides the sense.

John tried the same question in English.

"Note spik Inglish," replied the boy, haltingly, then he began drawing symbols on his palm.

John knew some Chinese characters, but he was by no means a fluent reader, for unlike the Roman alphabet with its twenty-six letters there are

26

thousands of individual characters in the Chinese language, and all have to be memorised.

No longer afraid of the Chinese boy, John took a ballpoint pen and a piece of paper from a drawer and offered them to the youth. The young man scribbled characters down on the paper and then handed it to John, who studied it for a few minutes. He recognised the character for 'hunger' and another for 'Beijing'. A thought struck him. The boy spoke another dialect, probably Mandarin. He was dishevelled and hungry. He had written the character for Beijing.

"You're an illegal immigrant, aren't you?" said John. "Where are you from? The north?"

The boy stared at him, failing to comprehend.

John took the bowl of rice out of his hands and into the living-room. He sat the youth down at the table, gave him some chop sticks, and indicated he should eat.

Then he went to the phone and dialled a number, while the youth watched him closely, eating at the same time.

"Jenny?" said John into the mouthpiece. "Can you come over to my place . . . I need some help."

"Now?" she said.

"If you could. Just for a few minutes."

"What is it? Homework? I'll have to ask my dad to drive me over."

"Okay, but make sure he stays in the car. Tell him you'll only be a few minutes and it's not worth him coming up."

"Why?"

"I can't explain now," said John. "Wait till you get here, but keep your dad downstairs."

"Okay," she said, sounding dubious.

When the doorbell rang fifteen minutes later the Chinese boy visibly jumped and panic sprang into his eyes.

"It's all right," said John in a calming voice. "It's okay. It's my friend. *Pang yau.* Understand?"

He let Jenny into the flat and quickly explained why he had asked her to come.

"I want you to translate this for me. He wrote it."

Jenny looked from John to the Chinese youth.

"That's not the one we saw today," she said, "out on the marshes. You sure he's not a burglar or something?" she asked.

"Jenny, you know as well as I do that there are dozens of them trying to get into Hong Kong every day. Read the note to me," insisted John.

Jenny scanned the characters and her eyes opened wide. Like John she only spoke Cantonese, but she was much more fluent than him in the written language. Finally she looked up.

"His name is Xu, and he's a student at Beijing University. He was in Tiananmen Square the night of the massacre, but escaped and came by train to Canton. He swam across from mainland China. He wants to know if we will hide him, because if he gets sent back they will execute him."

"I knew it," cried John, slamming his fist into his palm and making Xu jump again. "I knew he was an eye-eye."

"A what?"

"I.I. An illegal immigrant. What are we going to do with him? If we hand him over to the authorities they'll send him back."

Jenny said, "They wouldn't do that, would they?"

"They send eye-eyes back every day," John replied, "loads of them. And look what's happening to the Vietnamese refugees – they're talking about sending them back to Vietnam."

There was a refugee camp on the far side of the road from John's block of flats, and he could often see the brown-eyed children clinging to the chainlink fence, staring out at the world. Hong Kong was supposed to be a First Port of Asylum, where the boat people could rest before being transferred to countries prepared to take them in permanently, except that no country seemed to want them. They all talked a lot, and took a few refugees, but still there were many many thousands left to wait for years in the Hong Kong camps.

"That's different," said Jenny. "If Xu gets sent back, he may be killed."

"So could the Vietnamese. Look, you've read what the papers are saying. If Hong Kong is seen to be harbouring anyone taking part in the revolution, then China will accuse us of subversive activity. They'll stop being co-operative over the handover for 1997 and things like that. Most of our drinking water comes from China. They could cut it off, if they get angry . . ."

Jenny, too, knew that although the authorities

might want to be sympathetic, there was the possibility that the youth would be sent home to face trial. She had seen the boat people drifting into the harbour, being picked up by police launches. They had looked dreadful after their long sea voyages, possibly also having had to suffer being turned away by other countries, and yet all they were destined for was the refugee camps. Perhaps even if Xu was allowed to stay, he would be put into a camp?

"You're right," said Jenny, "we have to find a place for him to hide."

Chapter Four

"Where shall we hide him?" John asked. "We need to be able to get to him, so that we can take him food and water."

There was a place called Kowloon Walled City which, though it was in the middle of Hong Kong, was in principle still a part of China. Until the 1960s Hong Kong police had not been allowed to go in there, and the Chinese government was too far away to bother about it.

Kowloon Walled City was a giant slum, once full of illegal immigrants who could not be arrested. Some fifty thousand people lived in the Walled City, which no longer had a wall, but consisted of thrown together shacks, piled one on top of another, until there was a huge solid block of them, full of long dark corridors and thin musty air shafts. It had been a lawless place for many decades. Water from a few deep wells was a precious commodity. Though the majority of its inhabitants were decent people, it was a haven for criminals, illegal doctors and dentists, and the walls ran with moisture where they never dried out. There were rats and cockroaches by the thousand. People who lived in the middle never saw daylight. They roasted in the summer and chilled in the winter.

Nowadays, the police went in to arrest triad gangs, who robbed even the poor people of the slums. However, it was still the first place an eye-eye went to, since it was a maze. There were corners, nooks and crannies at the end of zig-zagging pitch black alleys where a man could hide forever and not be found.

"Shall we try the Walled City?" said Jenny. "I've been in a couple of times. I have a distant cousin who lives there."

John shook his head.

"I don't think that's a good idea. They're talking about pulling it down soon. Somewhere out in the country would be better. Up in the New Territories.

"There's a cave up on the Third Dragon."

John frowned.

"The Third Dragon?" Then he suddenly realised that Jenny was talking about the nine hills of Kowloon, and that the third one had a cave large enough for a youth like Xu to shelter in. "Oh, yes," he said excitedly. "Shall I take him up there?"

"In the dark?" said Jenny. "Rather you than me. Listen, I've got to get back to the car. My father will be wondering what's happened to me."

"Okay. See you at school tomorrow."

"Right."

Jenny left and John began gathering some things together, putting them in his rucksack. He took two torches, a loaf of bread and some cooked rice, two bottles of water and a blanket. The blanket wouldn't go in the rucksack, so he pushed it into Xu's hands. The boy from Beijing stared at it, not really understanding what was required of him. John hefted the pack on his back. It was quite heavy.

John said, "You come. *Nei lai*, okay?"

He pulled at the Chinese youth's sleeve, and motioned towards the door. Finally Xu seemed to grasp what they were doing and followed John out of the flat. They went down the service lift, to avoid meeting any residents, but the security guard was at the bottom washing one of the cars under lamplight. He stared at the two boys curiously, but John merely shouted "*Jo tau*" in greeting and hurried Xu by the man.

When they were about twenty yards away from the flats, John had a sudden thought.

"How did you get in?" he asked, staring back, for the Tenniel flat was on the top floor of the building, twelve storeys up.

Then he saw something dangling from the roof. A rope made out of strips of torn cloth. Xu had obviously tied some rags together, looped it around a TV aerial post, and lowered himself down onto the balcony to John's flat. The balcony doors had been

33

open, to let in the cool breezes and air the front room.

"Jeez," he said, "you took a risk. What if that makeshift rope had snapped? You'd have been a goner."

Xu jabbered something in Mandarin.

"Yes, well, whatever you're saying, it's a good job my dad wasn't at home, sitting in his favourite chair on the balcony," said John. "I don't think he'd appreciate Ninja's like you dropping down from the sky and invading his peace. He'd swallow his pipe."

John pinched the skin between thumb and forefinger on each side of his neck and pulled it out, showing Xu what his father would look like with a pipe stuck sideways in his gullet. Xu laughed, not really understanding, but knowing that John was making a joke of some kind.

The two boys crossed the busy Lung Cheung highway behind the buildings and onto the steep slope on the other side. There were no houses here, only scrubland covered in grass and bushes. John handed Xu one of the torches and indicated that he should switch it on. He used his own torch to light the way ahead, hoping no one was looking out of the back of the flats. They might report the moving lights to the police.

Climbing the hill was difficult, even by torchlight. For one thing John was terrified he was going to tread on a snake. There were several kinds in the scrubland, some of them poisonous. He knew that the venomous red-necked keelbacks were the most numerous, though they didn't often bite. If you trod on one,

34

however, it would be sure to retaliate.

The slope was slippery in one or two places, the dust having turned to mud where recent rains had not dried, or where small streams cut through the thin soil. Once or twice John had to grasp a bush to stop himself from sliding back, and he knew that Xu was having similar trouble.

It took twenty minutes to reach the cave, which looked dark and forbidding now they were close to it. John ran the torch beam over its floor and roof. There were one or two sizeable spiders and some geckos, but nothing more serious. So far as wild animals went, there were few to worry about. It was true there were wild boar, but they would not be so near a busy road. The next largest creature was the Chinese leopard cat which, though somewhat bigger than a domestic cat, was not known to attack humans. If Xu was to experience any serious problem, it would be with the monkeys, who might try to steal his food. They were extremely bold creatures that could inflict a nasty bite if annoyed. They roamed in packs, and the males were large enough to frighten any youth with sense.

Looking down from the cave, there was comfort to be had from the vast array of lights below. Yellow streetlights wound like jaundiced snakes through the high rise buildings and the narrow corridor of houses deliberately built low because they were in the flight path of the aircraft landing at Kai Tak airport. There were brilliant unblinking neon signs burning paths through the backstreets of Tsim Sha Tsui, and the buildings of Central were emblazoned with bright advertisements.

Indeed, almost the whole city could be seen stretching out as far as the Peak on the Hong Kong Island. It was a view many would have paid a ransom for, had they been allowed to build a house on the slope. In the near distance was Stonecutters' Island and beyond that Lamma, Cheung Chau and Lantau islands. Their lights were like sparkling jewels in the dark China Sea.

Then, just two hundred yards straight down, was the Lung Cheung Road with its constant flow of traffic. The roar could be heard quite plainly, even from within the cave. In the middle distance, the aircraft bound for Kai Tak, could be seen floating just above the rooftops as they came into land. It made John feel quite at home.

"You stay here," he motioned Xu. He passed the food and water to the Chinese youth and showed him that the blanket was for his bed. Xu was far from an idiot and though they spoke only in sign language, their understanding was soon very good. John indicated that Xu should not switch the torch on too often and when he did to turn it to face the mountainside, rather than Kowloon, where people might see it and report it.

Once he had settled Xu into his hideout, John began to descend by the slippery path, to the Lung Cheung Road beneath. Once there he switched off his own torch and waited for a gap in the traffic before dashing across the highway. There was a triple flight of stone stairs to go down, before John was on the same level as his block of flats, and he took these three at a time in his haste to be home before his parents. At the bottom of the steps was a dark corner, which John ran around . . . almost knocking over a man.

"Sorry," he said, in Cantonese.

The man looked taken aback. He was reasonably smartly dressed in shirtsleeves and long trousers, but there was something about him which disturbed John. Perhaps it was his eyes, which seemed jet black in the poor light? Or the sunken look to his cheeks, which might have been due to opium? He was like a giant stick insect, but his fingers were immensely strong as he gripped John by the elbow. He pushed his face into John's, exhaling the aroma of fried rice.

"Where are you going in such a rush?" said the man in Cantonese.

"Home. My flat is over there," said John, pointing. "I think I can see my father on the balcony."

He couldn't see anyone at all, and was reasonably sure his parents were still out, but the thin man worried him. The Chinese turned to look where John was pointing, still keeping a hold on his arm. As he did so, John saw what looked like the handle of a revolver sticking out of the man's back trouser pocket. He was thoroughly frightened now.

The man turned to him again, looking over John's shoulder into the alley that led to the flight of steps.

"Where have you been? I wish to know."

It was no good John feigning that he did not understand Cantonese, since the man had already

37

heard him speak it. He pointed to the Lung Cheung Road above them.

"Walking. I . . . I walked up to the lookout point, to see the aircraft landing at Kai Tak."

The man's eyes narrowed. It was a barely plausible story, but certainly a lot of boys were keen aircraft spotters and tried to outdo each other with their sightings.

"You speak good Cantonese. Are you an Australian boy?"

John suddenly became fed up with the way he was being questioned. He knew that on being accosted by someone, you shouldn't whine and blubber: it was better to become assertive. If you played the role of victim, then the person who was confronting you knew he had the upper hand. If you put on a no-nonsense front, however, you were more likely to make him think twice about what he was doing. That was the theory, anyway.

"English – some of me is. The rest is Chinese and if you don't let me go I'll call my father. He's a police chief at Kowloon Police Station. You can't molest people by grabbing them. That's illegal. You could go to prison."

Instead of dropping his arm, the man smiled, revealing a row of long browning teeth. His bony fingers were like steel-sprung claws on John's elbow.

"Is that so? And what might his name be?"

"I don't have to tell you that," said John. "Who are *you* if it comes to that? What are you doing, hanging around here? HELP! DAD!" He yelled with all the power of his lungs.

"Be quiet," snapped the man, but his grip relaxed slightly. "Earlier on I saw you with another youth – a Chinese boy . . ."

"Not me," said John. "We all look alike to you."

"Don't be funny," said the man, but then a light bus came up the hill and rounded the corner. It stopped and two Chinese men got off. They were dressed in suits: probably businessmen that had been working late. John filled his lungs to yell again, but his captor suddenly let him go.

"I'll be watching you," he said.

Then he strode away and jumped on the light bus.

John stood where he was, panting a little, partly from fright and partly from shouting. He did not want to run home until the man had gone, or he would know where he lived. So he waited until the light bus went past and then thumbed his nose at the face that stared at him from behind the window. There was a narrowing of the eyes, but nothing more. Then the man was gone.

When John was inside the flat, he found his parents were still not home. He switched on the television and watched the news, to see if anyone had reported seeing Xu. There was nothing about illegal immigrants, and he breathed a sigh of relief. There was, however, a political expert talking about what was going to happen prior to 1997 in Hong Kong, and one of the things he said made John sit up and listen.

". . . of course, the Chinese government in Beijing

will have already planted spies – secret police – here amongst us. They will be taking names, noting likely dissidents, for future reference. When they finally take over, the Beijing government will have a lot of information on people here, and I'm sure arrests will be made immediately."

China's secret police! Of course. That must have been what the man was! Why else would he be carrying a revolver? He must have been trailing Xu and then lost him when he got into John's flat. Then he had seen them together, briefly, but probably from a long way off, down the hill. By the time he had got to the top, John and Xu would have been over the highway and climbing the steep bank on the other side. It was doubtful the man had seen the torches, otherwise he would have confronted John with that information.

So the black-eyed man was obviously a mainland Chinese spy. A fifth-columnist as they sometimes called them. Perhaps John should report him to the police? But then he would have had to say what he himself was doing when the man confronted him. No, the best thing was to keep quiet about it all, and hope that he had seen the last of the secret agent.

Half an hour later his parents came in.

"Still up?" said his father. "Time you were in bed young man."

His mother, looking very regal in an evening dress, motioned for him to move towards the bathroom to get ready for bed.

"Okay," said John. "Did you both enjoy the play?"

"Your mother did," said his father.

"Your dad fell asleep," said his mother.

"I did not," came the inevitable protest.

"I hope he didn't snore, Mum, like the time he came to see the school play and all the other parents had to shush him."

"I did *not* fall asleep," cried his father in a hurt voice, and John and his mother laughed.

He liked to see his mum laugh. She had a naturally sad face, probably because she had had such a hard childhood in Macau, where her father was a minor clerk in some firm that exported fish. Her own mother ran away to Hong Kong when she was twelve and no one had heard from her since. John guessed that somewhere in the streets of Sham Shui Po or Wong Tai Sin, he might have sometime passed a wizened Chinese lady who was his grandmother, without even knowing her, or she him. It was an eerie and melancholy thought.

His dad said, "Right, that's enough jollity for one evening. Off you go to bed."

"I bet Alex stays up half the night," grumbled John.

"Not if Mrs Wilson has any say in it," said his mother.

"Well, even if he's in bed, he's probably boring his pal to death with his rotten jokes."

"They may be rotten to you, young man," said his

dad, "but I think our Alex may have a future as a comedian."

"Dad, that's because you don't have a sense of humour. Those jokes of his stink, honestly."

"Talking of stink," said his mother, "off you go to the bathroom, *now*. Wash, brush teeth and into bed."

John did as he was bid, glancing out of the back bathroom window to see if he could see a torch flashing on the hills above. All was dark and silent before the moon.

Just before climbing into bed, he remembered Xu's rope of rags, dangling from the roof. He sneaked out of the flat and retrieved this item, throwing it down the rubbish chute.

Chapter Five

At school the next day John met Jenny on the playing fields before assembly and told her what had happened after she'd left the previous evening.

"Xu is safely in the cave at the moment and I gave him enough food to last him until tonight, but we'll have to take turns in taking some up there for him."

"Peter will help," said Jenny. "He's a bit late this morning but we can see him at break."

"Okay, but don't let's talk about this in the classroom, or when anyone else is around. The man I saw last night could have spies in the school."

Jenny's eyes widened. "I'm sure none of the other kids would do anything like that."

John sighed. "Well, I'm not as sure about that as you seem to be. Anyway, we'd better go in. Old

Slimey's standing in the doorway looking at his watch."

They went inside the hall to sing some dusty hymns and listen to the headmaster chunter about smoking behind the outside toilets. He had caught a pupil from the fourth year, a girl by the name of Gwyneth Buntrum, having a cigarette during break. While he was talking, Peter crept in from the back, and took his place beside John.

"If I catch anyone smoking again," boomed the headmaster through the microphone, "they'll be expelled, and you have my word on that."

"Expelled," whispered Peter to John. "That's a bit drastic. What do they do if they catch you bunking off? Stretch you on the rack?"

"Patterson," growled Slimeball from behind, "see me before class."

"Yes, sir," said Peter, wearily.

"This is the colonies chum," whispered John in a much lower tone. "Punishment comes twice as fast and twice as hard out here. They're about as in touch with the real world as Wordsworth."

"Wordsworth's dead," said Jenny, automatically.

"Precisely," replied John.

Slimeball said, "Lee, Tenniel, you two as well. I know exactly what's going on in the *real* world, and if anyone says 'elephant ears' they'll remain with me after school."

No one spoke another word.

Just before assembly finished, Slimeball came up to the trio and said, "It was on the BBC world news this morning – they've caught Dick Turpin at last, on his way to York . . ."

It was a few minutes before the three friends realised that it was a joke. Slimeball was being humorous. The extra homework he gave them back in the classroom was not quite so funny.

At break the friends took themselves off to a corner of the playing fields and sat on the grass. Jenny told Peter what had happened the previous evening and asked him if he would help.

"Count me in," said Peter, "but what are we going to do in the long term?"

"What do you mean?" asked John.

"Well, we can't feed and water him forever. We've got to do something a bit more, I dunno, permanent with him. Find him some place where he can look after himself a bit more."

"What we've got to do," said Jenny, "is get him an identity card. Once he's got an ID, he can lose himself in Hong Kong. There's one or two little places where Mandarin is spoken. Xu will be able to make a new life for himself."

John said, "That sounds sense, but how do we get an ID card for him? Especially with this secret agent following us around."

"You've only seen him once," said Peter.

"Well, I know, but there are more of them. The man on the programme last night said there were probably hundreds of them in Hong Kong . . ."

Just then McAnders swaggered over to them. He was a big fourteen-year-old and as usual was accompanied by his cronies.

"Push off you lot," he said. "This is our turf."

"You've been watching too many late night films," Peter snapped. "What do you think you are, some kind of LA street gang?"

Rodin, another fourteen-year-old, put his face right up to Peter's and said, "You'll find out what we are, if you stand there any longer, sunshine."

"Nothing changes," muttered John, and Jenny said, "Come on, let's go."

"Pooh," said Peter, after the three had reluctantly left the corner to the bully boys, "his breath smelled of garlic."

After school Peter had to go down to Bird Street, in Mong Kok, to buy some live crickets for his father's pet bird. John went with him, taking the MTR underground, and they surfaced in the ethnic streets of the most densely populated area in the world.

The two boys hurled themselves into the bustling streets which were full of hawkers: people selling live fish from canvas water tanks, men selling live crabs with their claws bound with raffia, women selling live snakes and frogs.

A small, round-faced man sitting on a stool outside a shop, saw them walking through Mong Kok. He said something to a woman just inside the doorway, and set off in pursuit of the boys. This time he had a camera with him.

Peter and John made their way to Bird Street, which was just an alley full of sellers of caged birds.

Here also were the sellers of crickets: live food for pet birds.

"Disgusting," said Peter, holding his polythene purchase at arms length. The crickets hopped around inside the polythene, batting themselves against the transparent walls of the bag. "I don't know how my old man sleeps at night, feeding these poor things to that bird of his. It does nothing but screech anyway. I can't understand what he sees in it. Why can't we have a dog like any sensible family?"

"Because this is Hong Kong, that's why," replied John, as if that answered all and every question on the eccentricity of some parents.

Just at that point, John became aware that they were having their photograph taken.

"Hey?" he said, "What's this for?"

The round-faced man with the camera shrugged his shoulders and smiled.

"Tourist," he said. "I take pictures of birds. You just in the way."

Peter glowered at the man, who was now hiding behind a stall which dangled with bamboo bird cages.

"I don't like that," he said. "He doesn't look like a tourist to me. He looks like a policeman or something. I remember seeing him at the stadium the other day, during the demonstration. He was walking around with a notebook in his hand, and writing in it. He's probably gathering information on anyone who takes part in one of the rallies."

John's eyes widened.

"Now you come to mention it, I saw him too, only

47

later, outside the MTR station."

Peter, who was less inhibited that John, shouted, "Buzz off, you. Leave us alone. We're not doing anything wrong."

The man scowled and disappeared into the crowd clutching his camera.

"Flippin' cheek," muttered Peter. "People have got rights. It's an invasion of privacy."

"Let's forget it, Peter. We don't want to cause any trouble with the police. Come on. Not with Xu around."

Peter shrugged and the frown disappeared from his forehead. He changed the subject and asked John, "Has Jenny gone to see Xu?"

"Yes."

"Are you sure she'll be all right? She's only a girl you know."

"Whoa – say that to *her* and see how long you live."

Peter shrugged. "Well, I know, all this equality and everything, but that's for adults, isn't it? What I mean is, girls are not as tough as boys. Not physically."

"What do you think's going to happen?"

"Well," said Peter, "that secret copper, whatever he is. What if he sees her, follows her up the mountain and . . . well, you know, kills them both."

John's hair lifted on the back of his neck.

"*Kills* them?"

"It happens. You've only got to read the papers. There were two jewellry shop gangsters shot dead in Tsim Sha Tsui last night by the cops."

48

"Listen, Jenny will be fine," said John.

Nevertheless, what Peter had said disturbed him. It was true that while there was very little petty crime in Hong Kong, like bag-snatching or even mugging, major crime was not rare. Banks and jewellery shops were robbed at gunpoint relatively often, and murders were not unusual.

By the time he got home, he was quietly panicking. He said a brief hello to his mother, then went to his bedroom which overlooked the Third Dragon. Getting out his bird-watching binoculars, he scanned the hillside for signs of his friend, but found nothing. The cave was hidden by shrubs, but as he stared at it through the binoculars, John thought he could see some movement. He watched for some time, but then his mother called him to dinner, and he had to leave it.

On top of everything else, his mother caught him stealing a tart from the freezer, which he intended to take up to Xu the next day.

"What *are* you doing?" she asked.

"Um, it's the Festival of the Hungry Ghosts soon, isn't it? I was going to get this out ready to leave it for the spirits."

He was talking about a traditional day when Chinese families leave cakes and biscuits out for the ghosts of their ancestors. Yen Lo, the keeper of the Underworld always let the dead out for a romp on earth during the month of August and by the last day they were supposed to be starving, so people fed them before they went back down to the Underworld again.

"The Hungry Ghosts is not until August – we've got over a month to go," she said.

"Oh, really?" he feigned absentmindedness. "I thought it was much sooner than that. I'll put this back then."

His mother looked at him suspiciously, and took the tart from his hands.

"Never mind, I'll do it."

"Get to bed," yelled Alex from his own bedroom. "I wasn't allowed up so late at your age, ha, ha."

"You'll get a thick ear," cried John, already feeling very frustrated.

"It's thick enough, thanks. I don't want it to look like yours."

The next morning Jenny failed to turn up at school. Peter kept looking across at John with significantly raised eyebrows during class, and John's stomach was churning with anxiety. What if Peter had been right? What if Jenny had been kidnapped or something worse? He would never be able to look anyone in the eye again. It was all his fault for sending her up there without him.

Just when he was feeling at his most miserable, Jenny turned up, over two hours late.

She showed Slimeball a note.

"From my mother," she said, "saying why I'm late."

He gave it a cursory glance and nodded, pointing her to her place.

Jenny sat down without looking at either of the two boys and immediately began writing in her exercise book. She was a good student and Mr Ball had no reason to question her diligence.

At break time she told the two boys where she had been.

". . . to see my cousin in Kowloon Walled City. I've asked him to find someone to make a false ID card for Xu. Well," she confessed, "I said a passport at first, but my cousin said that was much too difficult or he would have made them for the family before now."

Like many Hong Kong Chinese, Jenny and her family wanted to emigrate before the Beijing government took over in 1997, but although her father had been a stoker in the British Navy for 20 years, and had been on the HMS Galahad when it was sunk in the Falklands' War, the family could not get British passports.

"An ID card's something, anyway. That'll be fine. We were worried about you though," said John. "Weren't we Peter?"

"Well, you were a bit anxious," replied his friend, "but I knew Jenny can take care of herself. I said to you, didn't I, 'Jenny's tougher than most boys I know. You don't need to concern yourself about Jenny . . .' "

John almost hit him.

"You great . . ." he began, but Peter interrupted with, "Steady lad. Don't say anything you might regret."

They both laughed, and Jenny looked mystified.

"What's this all about?" she asked.

"Nothing," laughed John. "Anyway, did you get

food to Xu last night? How is he? Did you take him some water?"

"He's fine," said Jenny. "He seems to have made himself quite comfortable. You would think he was used to camping out, though I suppose really he's got no choice. He was a bit scared of me at first."

"I can see why," interrupted Peter, "anyone would be, a great hulking monster like you."

Jenny ignored this and continued.

"He's made himself comfortable in the cave, with the blanket. I took him some other things up, that I found in our flat. A canvas stool and some newspapers."

"Which reminds me, how did you get your mum to sign the excuse note?" asked Peter. "Old Slimey didn't even want to read it."

"He couldn't," smiled Jenny, taking the note from her pocket and showing it them, "it's in Chinese."

The boys laughed when they saw the Chinese characters. Slimeball would never admit to not being as clever as his students and tried to give the impression that he could understand Hindi, Chinese, and Nepalese Gurkhali. Everyone went along with this to a certain extent, though none of them dared to ask a question in any of those languages, in case Slimey lost his temper with them. The Indians were the only children, other than British and Australian kids, who *might* challenge the teacher. The children of the Gurkahs were too afraid of authority, and the Chinese, like Jenny, too obedient.

"Your turn tonight Peter," said Jenny.

Peter turned slightly pale.

"Ah, look, I don't know the lad. I won't even recognise him."

"Easy," said John firmly, folding his arms, "he's the only one in the cave on the Third Dragon."

"No, what I mean to say is, he probably won't recognise *me*. He might do something silly, like run away into the . . . into the . . ."

"*Darkness*, is the word you're looking for," said Jenny.

"Yes," replied Peter, faintly. "Into the darkness."

John looked him squarely in the eyes.

"You're not *afraid* of going up there, are you Peter?"

"Me?" cried Peter. "*Afraid*?" He paused and then swallowed. "Well, just a *bit*. I don't mind the dark, you understand, but I'm not a good climber. I might lose my footing in the dark."

"I'd better come with you in that case," sighed John. "I know the path better than you do. All right?"

Peter gushed, "If you're going up yourself, you don't really need me, do you? I mean it's pointless *both* of us climbing up there, and I'll only get in the way, asking you things all the time. You know what I'm like. It's probably best you go alone."

"No it isn't," answered John. "We'll go together."

Peter seemed to resign himself to this.

"All right, but don't say I didn't warn you. I'm liable to get lost."

"I'll hold your hand," replied John.

"The hell you will," came back Peter in his John Wayne accent. "List-en Pil-grim, I can hold my own hand, all the way."

"Let's see if you can still be John Wayne while we're climbing up that dark path, with cobras all around us, a secret agent watching us through binoculars, and the chance of falling a hundred feet down on the Lung Cheung Road."

Peter put his arm around John and said to Jenny, "He's such a comfort to me, this boy."

She laughed.

Chapter Six

Xu was feeling homesick.

Below him lay the cityscape. In the harbour between Kowloon and Hong Kong Island, there were hundreds of boats of all sizes moving in seemingly haphazard fashion across the water: junks, ferries, lighters, sampans, tugs, barges, fishing smacks, yachts, military ships and launches, and further out in the bay, the cruise liners and cargo ships.

Not so long ago, only a few decades, the waters around Hong Kong had been infested with pirates. Even now there were still one or two pirate junks which preyed on trading vessels, coming swiftly out of the dark China sea, and waylaying some unarmed vessel on its way across the mouth of the Pearl River which separated Macau from Hong Kong. These days the pirate boats were driven by powerful engines which the family junks plying an honest trade could not afford.

In the myriad streets themselves was the dense traffic, which honked and clattered its way through every night and day, seemingly without a pause.

An aircraft passed overhead, flying low over the rooftops of the city.

Xu thought about trying to reach the airport and attempting to stow on board one of the planes. He had ventured down to the road below, once or twice, despite the warnings to stay in the cave. He decided to go down and have another look. It was boring on the hillside, with no one to talk to.

He scrambled down the slope and reached the highway. For a few moments he just stood there and stared at the lorries rumbling by, their drivers taking little notice of the Chinese youth. Then on impulse, when a gap appeared, he dashed over the road.

Once on the far side, Xu got a taste of freedom, and walked along the highway, heading for the docklands. All around the Kowloon peninsula were piers, jetties and docks. A ship, he thought to himself, would be easier to board than a plane.

Suddenly, he was amongst it all.

It was all noise, bustle and bluster – hooting ships, roaring traffic, thundering aircraft – and Xu was just not used to such a deafening blare of activity. Even in the great city of Beijing, the capital of China, there had been few cars on the road. Most people rode on bicycles. He was used to hearing very little but the sparrows.

He jostled his way along a pavement full of people like him. There were hundreds, thousands of shops, not like at home. Their goods spilled over, taking up pavement space. Colourful toys, pots and pans, luxury goods.

Xu stopped and stared into a fashion boutique, marvelling at the clothes he saw there. It was an Aladdin's cave of wonders to a youth who had to save many years to buy a single second-hand pair of jeans. There were shirts, slacks and jackets in abundance, and boys like himself were buying them, by ones, twos and threes. Where did such wealth come from? He felt himself flushing with excitement.

He was still bewitched by the scene when someone touched him on the arm and he looked round, directly into the face of a khaki-uniformed policeman. The man was glaring at him with the kind of eyes that only belong to people who see the worst in life. The policeman hooked his thumb under the strap of his Sam Browne and tipped his flat cap back on his head, while studying Xu's face.

Alarm swept through the student. Why had he left the cave? He should have stayed there, like the English boy had told him to. This place was full of enemies.

He was aware that the policeman was saying something to him in an angry voice. The girl, Jenny, had told him that they were trying to get him an identity card. This would be what the policeman wanted to see.

"Look at that!" cried Xu, pointing along the street, and then took to his heels in the opposite direction, crashing through boxes of oranges and apples, the owners of the fruit cursing him with shrill voices.

The policeman, who had not been fooled for a second, took off after him, yelling something. People scattered as Xu ran through them, knocking one or two off the pavement, into the road. He ducked quickly down a side street, looking back as he did so, and saw to his dismay that the policeman had drawn his revolver.

Xu reached the Lung Cheung Highway just as the policeman emerged from the crowded street. Without worrying about injury, Xu ran alongside a truck and jumped, clinging on to the side. He was thrown about like a rag for a few minutes, and sustained several hard knocks to his knees and thighs, but he managed to hold on. The policeman stood on the pavement, his hands on his hips, the revolver still in evidence. Xu was relieved that the man had not thought fit to use the weapon.

Xu dangled from the edge of the truck, in great danger of being thrown off at every corner around which it swerved. About a mile down the road, the truck driver suddenly saw him in the vehicle's side mirror, and stopped the truck abruptly. Xu jumped down, while the driver leaned out of his cab and yelled oaths at him in a stream of Cantonese, shaking his fist at the youth.

Xu dashed over to the far side of the road and continued running, along the darkened edge of the hillside, until he came once more to the path which led up to the cave. He did not understand this city of Hong Kong, full of Chinese like himself, but so utterly different to his own home.

Once in the safe environs of his hideout, Xu nursed his bruises, washing them with water and cooling their hurt. He stared out across the vast cityscape of Hong Kong, with its millions of lights, its skyscrapers. Everywhere ahead of him stood giant high risers, encrusted with lights.

Not for the first time he wished himself back in Beijing.

But Beijing was two thousand kilometres away.

Xu knew he could probably never go home now, to see his mother and father. He was their only child.

He found it terribly sad that his parents might die and he would not be there to see them suitably buried, or to help polish his grandfather's bones. Family is everything to a Chinese boy or girl, and Xu had lost his for good.

He couldn't help feeling utterly miserable when he thought of his father and mother. They had been so good to him, giving him an education even though they themselves had been illiterate. Now it seemed he had failed them in his attempt to obtain more freedoms for the people of China, and less corruption in the Chinese government. He was not sure it had all been worth it, for they seemed to be worse off than ever, since the protests.

There was a sound in the rocks below.

The English boy was coming with the food and water.

Chapter Seven

The man who was to do the fake identity card for Xu was a very careful person (so he told Jenny's cousin) and wanted to meet all three of them on neutral ground before agreeing to do the document. His name was Yeung Ng and he suggested that the temple at Wong Tai Sin might be an appropriate rendezvous point. However he told Jenny's cousin that he would need a photograph of Xu at the same time as agreeing to the task, so they were to take one with them.

Peter had a good camera which they could use, but time was very short. The trio were to meet Yeung Ng that evening at Wong Tai Sin and there was only half an hour between the end of school and the appointment.

"We'll have to bring Xu down to the MTR," said Jenny, "and use one of the quick photo machines. I've got fifteen dollars. That should be enough."

"Okay," John replied, as they walked down Suffolk Road, away from the school, "I'll go and fetch him. You two wait outside the MTR. I'll be about a quarter of an hour."

John dashed off then, and without bothering to go home, crossed the Lung Cheung Road and climbed the path to the cave. When he was halfway up, he remembered he should have got a note from Jenny, explaining to Xu what they were doing. Instead, when he got there, he had to explain to Xu in sign language, showing him is own ID card and pointing to the photo.

"You," said John, "same this!"

Eventually, Xu understood enough to know that he had to go with John somewhere, and followed him down the track. The Chinese boy was beginning to get very dirty and was starting to smell a little, so when they passed a public toilet, John took him inside.

"Wash," he said, making the motions.

Xu went to the washbasins and found a hard piece of old soap in the dish. It took him five minutes to have a rapid wash, during which time people came and went, but since many Chinese who had to work in the streets all day often came in to wash themselves, more or less all over, he didn't attract a great deal of attention. By the time Xu had finished, he looked quite presentable and at least did not smell of stale sweat any longer. Xu smiled at John and made a frame for his face with his thumbs and forefingers, indicating he was going to look handsome on his photo.

The two, aware that they were already late, hurried along the street to the MTR, where John received a shock. Standing on the corner, right outside the main entrance to the underground, was the secret agent, the spy from China. He was leaning against a wall, smoking a cigarette, fortunately looking in the opposite direction from which Xu and John had approached.

John pushed Xu down a side alley and put his fingers to his lips. They ran to the end of the alley and climbed the wall, John grazing his knees in the process. Once on the other side they were in the busy Waterloo Road, one of the arteries of the colony, and people and cars flowed past in their hundreds. They lost themselves in the crowd until they came to an MTR side entrance, out of sight of the spy.

A quick look satisfied John that the coast was clear and then he pushed Xu down the stairs to the escalator. He got him to a photo booth in the concourse above the level of the station platforms, and sat him inside.

"Wait there, don't move," he said.

The next thing to do was find Jenny and Peter, who didn't know what the secret agent looked like, and get them down to the concourse. John had asked the pair to meet him right outside the one entrance to the MTR that was guarded by their enemy. The only way he could think of reaching them, without being seen, was to go up the stairs to the main exit, right up behind the spy, and try to wave to attract their attention from behind his back.

John crept up the stairs at the top of which the Chinese spy was standing. The man was facing away from him. He was still smoking his cigarette and staring out into the crowd. John sneaked up behind him and with his heart in his mouth looked for Jenny and Peter amongst the people waiting for buses along the kerb. He saw them and waved frantically, praying that the man in front of him would not turn around. Eventually, Peter noticed John, and pointed.

John ducked down behind the stairs just an instant before the secret policeman turned. His heart was pounding like a drum in his chest and he was sure it could be heard. A few moments later Peter and Jenny appeared and the three of them ran down the stairs as if a monster were chasing them.

"Did he see you?" gasped John, when he felt they were safe.

"Did who see us?" asked Peter.

John said, "The spy, the secret agent. He was standing at the top of the stairs. That's why I couldn't come out."

"Oh, *him*," cried Jenny. "I wondered why he was looking at us like that. I thought I'd trodden on his toe or something."

"Did he seem as though he was going to follow you down?" asked John.

"No," replied Jenny. "I think he thought we were

waving to a family that came down just behind you, and went back to staring down the road."

John heaved a sigh of relief.

"I've got Xu in the booth. Have you got the fifteen bucks?"

Jenny gave him three five-dollar coins.

"Good. Let's get to it."

Xu posed for the photos as if he were on holiday in Thailand, and then, after a long wait, they had the photos in their hands.

"Peter, you take Xu back to the cave, while we go on to Wong Tai Sin. We'll have to explain to this Yeung fellow that you couldn't come. Use the far exit and then the back alley if you can, but be careful when you reach the other end as the spy can see you from there. Look out first, to make sure he's turned the other way."

"Okay," said Peter. "Come on Xu. *Lai*."

"He doesn't speak Cantonese," Jenny reminded Peter. "I think he knows more English than he does other Chinese dialects."

"Okay, well good luck to you two. See you later."

John and Jenny went down to the underground trains and caught the first one going to Wong Tai Sin. Once there, they went outside, following the signs to the temple. To get there they passed all the fortune tellers who had their booths outside the temple's close. They were there to interpret the "lucky stick" numbers that devotees brought to them after a session in the temple. People would go down on their knees before the altar of a god and shake a canister full of sticks with numbers on them, until two or three fell out. These they would note on a piece of paper, then go to a fortune teller outside the gates to have the numbers interpreted.

Wong Tai Sin Temple, like many temples in Hong Kong, was a working temple, used by the populace that lived in the high-rise blocks of council flats that surrounded and overshadowed it. Unlike the show-piece temples of Thailand, it was well used and always had lots of people milling around inside its courtyards, with the consequent rubbish littering the floor: orange peel, used joss sticks, newspapers (used for kneeling on) and offerings of chicken and fruit that had been knocked over. There was bustle and noise, and lots of colour: gold for the gods, red and yellow for luck. There were murmurings and mutterings and low bee-like humming as pious Chinese prayed to their various gods. There was the ever-present fragrance of incense, like strong perfume in the air, as joss was burned, some of it in the form of great coils of inch-thick cable, dangling from the ceiling of the temple in spiral cones.

The pair met Yeung Ng in the Garden of the Nine Dragons Wall, overlooked by thousands of bamboo poles of clean washing, hanging out like flags of poor nations from the windows of council flats. Beyond the flag-bedecked buildings was the Lion Rock, which from that angle did indeed look like a lion resting outside its cave.

Yeung Ng was standing on an ornamental bridge, looking down into the waters of the lotus pool at the koi carp swimming through the green plants. John and Jenny joined him.

The first thing Yeung Ng said made their hearts sink.

"Have you brought the money?"

"We haven't even agreed a price yet," said Jenny, despair in her voice. "I thought you might do it for nothing, since it's for a good cause."

Ng's face tightened.

"I don't do things for nothing," he said, in Cantonese. "Where's your third member. Has he got the money?"

"No," said John, "he couldn't come."

Ng's eyes tightened, but he did not turn and walk away. He seemed to believe them. He shook his head slowly as if acknowledging as much. "I'll tell you what, I am prepared to reduce my price to help someone from China. I came from China myself, when I was eight. One fake ID card, right? This will cost you . . ." he took out a calculator and like most Chinese shop salesmen do, appeared to calculate the cost of the job, though he probably knew what he wanted to charge all along. Once he had finished punching the keys, instead of telling them, he showed them the figure.

"Eight hundred dollars?" cried John in English. "We can't afford that! *Tai gwai. Peng di, dak m'dak – aaa?*" he added, asking Ng to make it cheaper.

Ng pursed his lips.

"For you, special price," he said, using English to save face because John had used Cantonese, and banged away on the calculator again.

He showed it to them. Three hundred dollars.

"*Ey-yaa*," cried Jenny, in the typical Cantonese way of showing disapproval.

Eventually they got it down to two hundred and forty dollars, which was about twenty pounds in English currency. They then had to confess that they had no money with them at the time, which didn't seem to disturb Ng in the least.

"I make ID card," he said in English, "then you bring money to me in Kowloon City, okay? You got photo?"

They gave him the strip of four photos.

Yeung Ng left the Nine Dragon's Garden first, and the other two followed later. There was a uniformed policeman outside the temple but he took no notice of the two youngsters, as they hurried through the avenue of fortune tellers, to the MTR.

When they got back to Kowloon Tong station, the spy was still there, lounging against the corner of the east exit. The Chinese have infinite patience in carrying out such things and John would not have been surprised if the man was still there next Monday morning, when they went to school.

"Goodnight Jenny," said John, when they had again left by the west exit and climbed the wall to the alley.

She wished him good night and they parted.

A round-faced man with a notebook in his hands watched them go towards their separate homes. Since being seen in Bird Street, the man had kept well out of sight when following the youngsters. He followed many people in Hong Kong, especially those whom he believed would be useful to him one day. The man was not really interested in Peter, because he was a *gwailo* and would be leaving Hong Kong before the Chinese government took over, but John had Chinese blood in him, and Jenny was fully Chinese. These two might stay on and might be college students by that time. Students are often the cause of unrest in a country. They challenge governments. It was best to keep dossiers on students that were likely to cause trouble.

John ran up the steep hill to his home. He was already late and he knew his father hated meal times to be delayed. When he got in they were just serving up, however, his mother having been held up too at Lok Foo shopping centre, where she had gone for the fish for the meal.

"Made it by the skin of your teeth," said his father. "Where have you been, anyway."

"Wong Tai Sin temple," replied John, seeing no reason not to tell the truth.

"What on earth for?" asked his mother, who was always surprised when her family took any interest in Chinese culture. Since she had grown up with it, she took it for granted, and saw nothing exotic in it at all. Though the two boys had been raised in Hong Kong, they had also spent a lot of time in England with their British grandparents, and knew in what fascination westerners held the orient.

"Oh, I like to go down there every so often,"

confessed John. "It's full of noise and bustle."

"You could have stayed here and got some noise," crowed Alex, lounging on a bean bag that he had all but destroyed with his leaps and pummels, "Dad's been bashing nails in the wall and Mum's been bustling – I'm the only quiet one."

Dad pointed a finger at him.

"You don't be so cheeky my lad."

"It's good for me to have my own opinions," said Alex. "I show a healthy regard for freedom of speech. You're going to need people like me in 1997, when the Chinese take over."

Mum raised her eyes to the ceiling.

"Ten years old and he's a politician."

"In 1997," replied Dad, "we shall be long gone from here. Not that I want us to go mind, but we shan't be welcome, I don't suppose."

John said, "I don't like that. This is my home."

"Well, you'll be nineteen when that day comes, so I suppose able to make your own decisions on whether to go or stay. Personally, I hope you come with us, but I won't force you."

The children's mother had gone quite pale. Discussions about the family splitting up always disturbed her, probably because of her own family history.

"Dinner's ready," she said.

On the news that evening there was a programme about the Phoenix Refugee Camp, where some of the thousands of Vietnamese boat people were kept. John recalled the time he had taken his cycling certificate out on the disused airfield at Sek Kong. Part of the airfield had been wired-off and used as a refugee camp. One of John's classmates had complained about the smell that was wafting from the camp at the time.

The teacher who was with the class became very angry with the boy.

"Look at that place," he told the whole class.

John and the others did as they were told, seeing children like themselves hanging listlessly on the chainlink fence, staring out at them with large envious eyes. Inside the wire there was a desultory game of football in progress, the players using an old tennis ball, but John sensed the futility of the children there. The concrete runway, bare and baking hot, was their permanent home.

"You want to change places?" the teacher had asked the boy. "You said you didn't like the smell. How would you smell if you lived in a place like that, with inadequate facilities for washing and going to the toilet? Not so sweet, I imagine. I see you've brought a towel with you, to rub yourself dry when you get sweaty. Those people have to use rags when they get chance to shower. That's if they're lucky. Most of them have to dry off in the sun."

"Yes, sir," said the boy, thoroughly contrite.

The image of those Vietnamese children, on that day, had left a strong impression in John's mind. He knew how fortunate he was to be on the other side of that wire. He had seen the boats come in, by Stonecutter's Island, with the Vietnamese on board draped over the gunwhales looking dehydrated, close to exhaustion, perhaps even death. They had fled one nightmare, to find another waiting for them.

One thing became clear to John, however, as the programme proceeded: that people in Hong Kong were fed up with illegal immigrants, even though they may have been such themselves not so long ago, and if Xu were discovered he might very well be sent back to China. At least he stood a better chance than the Vietnamese, whose cause may have been taken up by human rights organisations, but whose presence in Hong Kong aroused irrational resentment amongst the Chinese population.

He was at least Chinese, if not Cantonese. It would have been better if he had come from the south, not the north of China, but he was a Han and nothing could change that. A Han would not be treated as favourably as a Cantonese or Hakka, or one of the southern peoples, but he stood a better chance than a Vietnamese.

"What a mess," sighed John. "Why did God make us all look and speak differently, have different ways? Why couldn't he have made us all the same? Then there wouldn't be any arguments."

His father caught the gist of this, though of course he had not known the thoughts behind it.

"Wouldn't have made any difference son. People will disagree, argue and fight over things until the world comes to an end."

"But who is it wants to fight? I don't," said John, "nor do you or Mum."

"I do," said Alex. "I want to be Batman and smash crime."

"Be serious a minute, Alex," said Dad. Then turning to John, he said, "Most people just want to get on with their lives. Unfortunately, some are not allowed to and begin to fight in order to get out of that situation. Others want power, and fight for that reason alone. You would like it to be simple – so would I – but unfortunately humans are complex animals."

"I guess so," said John. "Anyway, I've got home-work to do. What about you, Alex?"

"Oh, thanks for reminding me," cried Alex in a sarcastic tone. "Thanks very much, bruv, or I would have forgotten and then where would I be? Prob'ly watching that fantastic cowboy film on TV in a few minutes' time. *That* would be a waste of brains, wouldn't it?"

John smiled. His brother Alex was incorrigible, but he was fond of him just the same.

Chapter Eight

John, Peter and Jenny's next big problem was where to get the money for the fake ID. It wasn't an *enormous* amount, but they couldn't take $240 out of what they already had in their individual savings.

"How much can you afford, Peter?" asked John.

"Sixty dollars, tops. My parents keep eagle eyes on my savings account. Any more than that, and they'll think I'm buying an air rifle, or something."

"Well, I can match that. What about you, Jen?"

Jenny shook her head sadly.

"At the moment, I can only get about forty dollars."

The three friends were sitting on a bench in Shek Kip Mei Park, watching the koi swim dangerously close to the ornamental waterfall that had a twenty-foot drop to the pool below.

"That leaves us eighty dollars short," said John. "Any suggestions? Can we borrow it?"

"No chance," said Peter. "We can't ask an adult for it and if we try going round the school kids, we'll arouse suspicion. McAnders already knows there's something going on, and he keeps giving us funny looks. You know what him and his cronies are like, when they latch on to something."

"What about a raffle?" said Jenny.

"Illegal, unless you get a license, and somehow I don't think they'll give one to a bunch of kids," said Peter.

Jenny snorted. "Do you think buying ID cards is any more legal?"

John asked, "What would we raffle? I haven't got anything that's worth eighty dollars."

"It doesn't have to be worth eighty for us to make that much in a raffle. It need only be worth ten, but we stand much more chance of making eighty, *if* it's something other kids want. Something that appeals to both girls and blokes."

This was from Peter who, true to form, once his objection concerning legality had been swept aside, dived head first into the project.

"I've got a camera," said Jenny. "It's about a year old. My parents gave it to me, but it won't really be missed until we go on holiday, in December."

John was a bit worried by this.

"But Jenny, what happens when they *do* find out?"

"I'll . . . I'll tell them it's lost," she said.

"No you won't," interrupted Peter, "I know you. You couldn't lie directly to your parents if you tried, Jenny. Listen, I have a Swiss Army knife, my uncle Dave gave me. My mum and dad hate it. They think I'm going to chop my leg off by accident with it some day. It won't be missed at all. They'll think I've mislaid it and heave a sigh of relief, hoping I won't find it again. They certainly won't mention it. Swiss Army knives are pretty expensive items."

John said, "This is pretty good of you, Pete. I mean, you're already putting in more money than us two."

Peter swelled his chest a little.

"Think nothing of it, chum," he said.

Then he glanced at the other two sideways.

"Since I am putting in the lion's share," Peter muttered, "maybe . . . maybe one of you could do my turn and carry the food up to Xu, just to make it even out a little?"

"No," replied John, "but *good* try, all the same."

Jenny laughed at them.

Just then, two older boys swung through the gateway to the park and came sauntering in with their hands in their pockets. They saw the trio and made straight for them. It was McAnders and Bailey.

McAnders grinned at them.

"G'day," he said in a broad Australian accent.

"Hello," replied John, warily.

Bailey, a tough English boy, the son of a Regimental Sergeant Major in the Royal Engineers, said, "Well, well, what have we here? Plotting against your elders? Revolution, is it?

"Don't know what you're talking about, Bailey," said Peter.

McAnders face grew dark. "Don't you, mate? Well maybe a thump in the head might improve your understanding."

The two bigger boys barred the way, as the trio made preparations to leave. John had been knocked about by McAnders and Bailey before and really did not want it to happen again. He was also getting worried about Xu, who would be expecting someone with water and food. However, the two thugs were not going to get out of the way, that was obvious.

McAnders said, "Before you go, mate, you can tell us what you three are up to. You think I'm daft? I know you've got something going on. I want to know what it is."

There was a Mexican standoff for a few moments, with one side staring into the other side's faces.

Finally, Jenny broke the silence.

"I'm going," she said, and took a step forward.

"No you ain't," said McAnders moving in front of her.

Jenny looked at him with angry narrowed eyes.

"You *dare* touch me?" she snapped. "I'm Chinese. We don't play boy's games. One finger on me and the whole Lee clan will be looking for you, you understand that, *gwailo*? You know how many Lees there are in Hong Kong?"

McAnders moved his head back from the glaring girl, as if he were feeling the heat of a fierce fire. He stood there for another second and then grinned, before stepping aside.

"Who cares . . ."

Jenny left them and walked quickly out of the park.

Peter stepped forward, but Bailey said, "You two ain't goin' anywhere. There's no clan to protect *you* boys."

Jenny broke into a run as soon as she was out of the boys' sight and could do so without losing face. She was concerned about Peter and John, but if she called their parents, they would not like it, she knew that. In any case, once adults were brought on the scene, there would be questions asked, and eventually the truth would come out about Xu. She decided it was better she go home, get some food and water, and take it up to the cave. Otherwise Xu might get restless, thinking no one was going to come, and set off in search of them himself.

When she reached home, only Tess, the Filipina amah, was in the house. Her father was still at work, she knew, but her mother was normally around. She spoke in English because Tess understood that language better than Cantonese.

"Tess," she asked the amah, "where's Mother?"

"She's gone out, Jenny. She won't be back until seven-thirty. She said you are to get on with your homework. If you like, I'll give you some help."

Tess had looked after her since she was a little girl, and although the Filipina maid was a house servant she was well educated. She worked in Hong Kong because jobs in the Philippines were difficult to get.

"I've got to go out to see a friend," said Jenny. "I won't be long."

Tess gave her a sideways glance.

"That's not like you, Jenny. You always like to get your homework done first."

"I know. This . . . this is urgent. I just want something to eat before I go."

"What? You want your mother to shout at me? You have to wait until dinner, or I'll be in trouble."

Jenny knew there would be no budging Tess, once she folded her arms in that manner. Tess was barely an inch taller than Jenny herself, but the Filipina was stocky and formidable. Not that Tess would lay a finger on her, but Jenny was typical of many Chinese children in that she was obedient to adults to a degree which mystified some European teenagers.

So Jenny left the flat. She had seven dollars in her pocket and raced round to the nearest street hawker stall, where she could buy take-away food right there on the pavement. In certain districts in Hong Kong, hawker stalls abound, selling noodle and rice dishes cooked according to secret clan recipes. The food was very cheap, though even the drivers of Rolls Royce cars stopped at their favourite stalls on their way home to dinner. She found a man cooking chicken-rice in a gas-heated great iron wok of ancient origin, which looked blacker and greasier than a range in a Victorian England kitchen. She asked for four dollars' worth of chicken-rice, and the stall owner grinned at her showing several teeth missing in his gaunt face.

"Sei man? Hai!" he said, agreeing.

He stir-fried the chicken-rice with a flourish, the flames from the gas ring licking up around his arms as if to engulf him, when the fat splashed over the rim of the wok. Jenny wished he would hurry up. For once she began to get impatient of the showmanship that went with a meal from the hawker stalls. Unfortunately, that was all in the price, and expected of the cooks, so they knew no other way to prepare the food. At one point she thought he was going to set himself on fire, he was so nonchalant with the flames.

Finally the rice was done and put into a polystyrene box for her to carry away. A set of softwood chopsticks went with it.

The food in her hand, Jenny then dashed into the nearest soft drink shop and bought a bottle of Chinese spring water. Then she made for the Lung Cheung Road.

By the time she began to climb up the narrow path to the cave, it was quite dark. The shadows of the day had retreated into their hiding places under the rocks and the bushes had taken on unfamiliar shapes. Jenny had to struggle in one or two places, to keep her footing, but finally she reached the cave.

"Xu?" she called softly, and when there was no reply, more loudly, "Xu? Are you there?"

Receiving no answer she went to the mouth of the cave.

"Xu? Are you in there?"

Silence. The wind played in the grasses about the dark mouth of the cave. She entered the cave cautiously, thinking he might have dropped off into a deep slumber. It was pitch black inside.

"Xu? Are you asleep?"

Suddenly something whipped through the darkness like a snake and gripped her arm tightly. Hot stinking breath hit her nostrils, making her stomach turn over. She felt strands of greasy hair or rags flapping against her cheek as a face was thrust against hers.

"*Bin goh nei?*" screeched a shrill, deafening voice. "*Bin goh nei?*"

Jenny screamed.

Peter and John had watched Jenny leave Shek Kip Mei park with relief. At least someone would now be able to get to Xu and take him his food and water. Still, there were McAnders and Bailey to deal with, and the two bigger boys were very formidable opponents. Neither Peter nor John were a match for them and they knew their only chance to escape was to bluff their way out.

"Well," snarled McAnders, "I'm waitin' for an answer, unless you want your head punched in?"

"All right, you win," said Peter, and John looked at him, alarmed. Peter shrugged. "We've got to tell them," he said. "I don't want my head punched in."

"Yeah," said Bailey. "So what is this conspiracy?"

Peter said, "It's not a conspiracy, not as such. You know this clothes collection all the classes are doing for the Vietnamese refugees?"

This much was true. It had developed into a

competition between classes and Mr Ball was keen his class should collect the most cast-offs to hand to the central committee that was sorting and delivering the clothes directly to the camps.

Bailey nodded, cautiously, his eyes narrowed.

"Well, Jenny Lee, John and me are planning to go round the Army married quarters. The Forces families only stay two years, so there are always people getting ready to leave Hong Kong. They often get rid of a whole pile of stuff before they go, to save on packing and storage. We reckon we can win the competition."

McAnders snorted.

"Is that all? I don't believe it. You've got something else cooking."

"Scout's honour," said John, giving the scout's three-fingered salute.

"Boy scouts," sneered Bailey. "I might have guessed as much. Dib dib dib."

"Wrong," said Peter, flaring in protection of his favourite pastime. "That's the cubs. When we're called to order, we shout 'Troop'."

McAnders glared at him.

"I don't care if you shout 'turnip soup'," he said.

Just at that moment, John's eyes widened, for walking along the pavement outside the park looking very lost, was Xu.

"Anyway, we've got to go," he said to the two bigger boys.

"Not so fast," said McAnders, but John was already pushing past him. McAnders stuck out his foot, so John tripped and sprawled on the concrete. Bailey laughed.

"Just watch it in future, Tenniel, and you, Patterson," Bailey said, "stay away from the barracks. *I'm* the army brat here. That's *our* territory. If there's any clothes to get there, we'll get 'em. Savvy?"

Peter nodded, sullenly.

With that they slouched off.

Peter helped John to his feet.

"I'm going to get that McAnders one day," he said, "and I know just who to see about it."

"Who?" asked John.

"His younger brother, Sam. Sam McAnders is a good mate of mine. He once told me there's something McAnders is scared of, and that's how he always gets his big brother back when he's bullied. I'm going to find out what that something is – and use it. I hope it's snakes. I'd love to put a big fat rat snake in McAnders' desk."

"Well never mind about that now," said John, beginning to panic. "The reason I got brave was because I saw Xu. He was wandering along the pavement outside. We've got to get to him, before he lands in any trouble . . ."

"Xu?"

"Yes, come on!"

The two boys raced through the park gates and down the hill towards the Kowloon-Canton railway station. They passed the new polytechnic college at breakneck speed, but still there was no Xu in sight.

"Where's he got to?" gasped John, pausing for breath.

"Are you *sure* it was him?" asked Peter.

"Absolutely certain. He had that lost-in-the-forest look on his face. I couldn't be mistaken. Come on. He must have gone down to the KCR station. Let's go up on the bridge and see if we can see him from there."

They took the steps descending to the footbridge over the railway three at a time, but when they got to the bottom and overlooked the platforms, now lit in the closing dusk, there was a seething mass of black-haired Chinese commuters, waiting for trains to the New Territories and China itself.

"Can you see him?" asked John, anxiously.

"Fat chance," said Peter. "It's like looking for a single straw in a haystack. How could we recognise him amongst that lot. There's thousands of people down there."

John groaned.

"Well, what are we going to do?"

"One thing's for sure, he hasn't got any money, so he can't catch a train. I vote we stand here for the next few minutes, watch a couple of trains come and go, and hope we can spot him as the platforms empty."

"On the other hand, he might not even *be* down there."

"True. *You* stay here. I'll scour the roads nearby and see if he's tucked away in an alley somewhere. Won't be long."

Peter raced away to do his search.

John remained on the bridge, not very hopeful of success.

Chapter Nine

After half an hour of searching, it became obvious that they were not going to find Xu amongst the crowds, and the two boys made their way to a news stand outside the station. Calls within Hong Kong were free, so the newsagent did not mind them using his telephone, and John called Jenny's home.

"Hello?" said a voice in English.

"Hello, is that Tess? John Tenniel here. I wonder if I could speak to Jenny, please?"

Tess sounded worried.

"She's not in at the moment, John. She went out some time ago and hasn't been back. I'm a little bit concerned . . ."

John's heart did a flip.

"Oh, okay Tess. Well, if we see her – Peter

Patterson is with me – we'll tell her you're anxious and to go home."

"Yes please, thank you John."

John put the phone down and stared at Peter.

Peter said, "What?"

"Jenny's not home yet."

"Well that could mean anything."

"Yes," said John, "but we know she's probably gone up to feed and water Xu, and where's Xu?"

Peter's brow wrinkled.

"Down here!"

"Right," said John, "but *why*? Don't you think he might have been scared away from the cave by something? I don't think it can have been the spy, because he would have captured Xu, wouldn't he? Likewise, the police would have taken him into custody. It would be difficult for anyone to run away up there. There's nowhere to go but down, and if someone was coming *up* – you see what I mean?"

"So what do you think scared him?" asked Peter. "Wild boar? Leopard cat? Snake?"

"Not many boars and cats around, but there's plenty of snakes. What if Jenny's up there now, having been bitten? She might be lying on the cave floor, unconscious or something. We've got to go up there Peter, *now*."

"Now," repeated Peter, with a touch of fatalism in his voice, as if he never expected to see his parents again.

"We should take something with us," said John.

"Do you have any firecrackers left from our visit to Macau?"

The boys had smuggled firecrackers, used for religious festivals by the Chinese, into Hong Kong. Firecrackers had been illegal in Hong Kong itself since the riots in an earlier decade, when they had been supposedly used to cover the sound of gunfire. Still, out in the New Territories the farming villages and fisherfolk sometimes still let strings of them off, risking fines from the courts, and if anyone other than the police heard them they would think there was some kind of ceremony going on. A lion dance, or something.

"My place," said Peter, gloomily, "at least I can say goodbye to Mum and Dad."

"Don't be such a doom merchant," replied John. "We'll be okay. It's Jenny I'm worried about."

The two boys went to Peter's flat and made quick small talk with Peter's parents, before sneaking to his bedroom and grabbing the string of firecrackers from his secret hiding place behind the wardrobe. There were about fifty in the bunch, looking like a bandolier of red shotgun cartridges, strung together in two adjacent lines. Matches were obtained from the kitchen, as well as two torches. The boys also took a set of small lion dance cymbals and some Tibetan prayer bells. They then got to the front door without being seen.

"Just going round to John's," Peter called. "Got a bit of homework to sort out."

"Don't be late," returned his mother.

"Okay."

They raced down the road and to the foot of the Third Dragon, then climbed silently and swiftly to the cave, feeling like commandoes on a deadly mission. To the left and below them there was some sort of commotion going on in the Phoenix Vietnamese refugee camp, but they had no time for wondering. They had a job to do.

As they climbed, John was vaguely aware that the temperature had dropped considerably, and a strong wind was rustling the bushes, lifting the grasses.

When they reached the cave, they crept around the side of it and climbed up above it, where there was a hole the size of a street drain in the roof. They planned to frighten the snake, or whatever it was, out through the front opening of the cave. Then they could go in safely and look for Jenny. Both of them were dreading what they might find and were feeling very guilty for getting Jenny into trouble in the first place.

John lit the fuse to the firecrackers and dropped the hissing bandolier down the hole. After two seconds there was the most almighty string of explosions, sounding louder than a machine gun in the hollow rock cave. Then the two boys began yelling and screaming, John clashing the cymbals, and Peter clanging the prayer bells. There was enough noise to give an elephant a heart attack, let alone chase some small creature from the darkness of its lair.

"Whooo, whooo, whooo," shouted Peter.

"Yaaah, Yaaaaaaaaaaaaaah," cried John.

"Aaaaaaeeerrrhhhh!" screamed someone from inside the cave, and the next moment a figure hurtled through the front opening and went tumbling head over heels, down the slope for about twelve yards, before coming to rest in some bushes. There the figure lay moaning, its arms wrapped around its head, as if warding off demons. It had formed naturally into a foetus shape and was rocking itself back and forth, perilously close to falling down the edge of a cliff to the road beneath.

John was so startled by this result, he almost ran away too. It was as if they had flushed the Devil himself from the depths of the earth. Peter had clutched his arm and, without realising, was squeezing hard enough to bring tears to John's eyes. John prised away Peter's fingers. Then the two boys, with their hearts lodged in their throats, climbed down the rocks to where the figure was rolling and whimpering, and shone their torches at it.

It was only a man in a ragged brown dust coat, such as those worn by stockmen in supermarkets, or assistants in hardware shops. He was a rather pathetic-looking man with thin limbs and a bony body. He was extremely dirty and his long black locks which he protected with his arms, were matted into greasy ropes of hair. A ragged black beard trailed from his chin and was lifted almost horizontal by the wind. There were sandals on his feet, held together by nylon packing string.

His Chinese features emerged and were caught in the torchlight.

John lowered his torch and said with some relief in his voice, "It's only old Yam Yam."

The man they had frightened half to death was a local tramp, who lived some of the time in his giant cardboard box in a covered walkway at Central, but occasionally went wandering up through Kowloon. He kept himself alive by searching the rubbish bins in the street for take-away cartons, which invariably still had some rice or noodles in the bottom.

"Yam, Yam, what are you doing here?" asked John in Cantonese, taking the torch out of the old man's eyes and shining it on himself and Peter, so that Yam Yam could see there was nothing to be concerned about.

"Ahh. You two boys. I know you two boys."

Yam Yam pointed a finger at them.

Peter said in English, "Have you seen a young girl?"

Yam Yam smiled.

"Ah. Missy come. Missy give Yam Yam some food and water. Missy nice girl." His face changed its expression. "Then ghosts come. Shout, shout, shout. Tell Yam Yam to get out of cave. Ghosts very noisy. Go BANG BANG BANG! Go YA YA YA!" He yelled at the top of his voice and then looked around at the cave with wide and wondering eyes.

"That was only us, Yam Yam," said Peter. "We thought there was a snake in the cave. Where's missy now?"

Yam Yam reverted to Cantonese, addressing his remarks to John, who he knew understood his language better than Peter.

"The girl went home," he said.

Suddenly a third and very powerful torch lit the three figures and all them turned their heads to look into bright light. They could see nothing of course, but a shining beam which had them shielding their eyes.

"Who's that? Is that you, Jenny?" asked John.

"No, it's not," said a male voice from behind the light.

Once the light was taken out of his eyes and he had a few moments to adjust, John saw who the owner of the voice was, and his flesh began to crawl.

It was the mainland Chinese spy.

"What are you three doing here?" asked the man in good English, his coat flapping as he stood on a pinnacle of rock in the full force of the wind.

"Free country," said John.

"That it's not," said the man. "It happens, at the moment, to be a British colony, not a free country."

"What I mean is," said John, taken aback, "that we can go where we like, so long as it's not against the law."

"Did you know there's been a breakout in the Phoenix camp below? This hillside is covered with policemen at this time, looking for escaped refugees."

That indeed was an alarming piece of news.

Peter said, "I don't blame 'em."

"What? Who don't you blame?" asked the man.

"The refugees. It's like a concentration camp, that place. They're prisoners there. I'd break out, if I was one of them."

"Some of them are bad people," said the man.

"There are *bad* people everywhere," replied John, with a significant nod at the spy.

The man waved his hand impatiently.

"In any case," he said, "I still want to know what the three of you are doing here. I can make you talk to me, you know."

His tone was threatening. John remembered the gun he had seen the man carrying and guessed he would still have it.

"Nothin'," said Peter, sullenly. "We're not doing anything."

"Nothing indeed," cried the man, waving his torch at them. "You've been bringing food and water up here for at least two days. I've seen you. Who was it for, this wretch?"

Yam Yam nodded vigorously, saying, "Thank you, thank you."

"Yes," replied John, "it was for Yam Yam. He'd starve up here. He's a bit simple, you see. When he's down in the streets he scavenges from bins, but he doesn't realise there's no bins up here, so we bring him things. Any harm in that?"

The man stared at them as if sifting the truth from this statement. In the light of the torches his face was a mass of hard shadows. There was a brittleness to him which was in his movements, in his appearance, in his voice. It would not have surprised John if someone had told him this man was not human, but was a robot, or a puppet.

Finally the man spoke again.

"I suggest you go down from here and return to your homes. If I find you're not telling the truth you will be in serious trouble, do you understand? I shall be watching you two like a hawk."

The two boys nodded.

"Off you go then," said the man, waving his torch at them.

"What about Yam Yam?" said John, stubbornly. "We're not leaving him here."

"Why not? He's been up here nearly a week, hasn't he?"

"Yes, but if you're going to stop us coming here, Yam Yam will starve," said Peter.

The man gave a snort of disgust.

"He won't *starve*. When he gets hungry he'll go looking elsewhere for food."

John took his courage in both hands.

"Well, I don't care what you say, mister, because I'm going to keep bringing food for Yam Yam. You *can't* stop us coming here. It's a Country Park."

The man drew back.

"You're a very impolite young boy, aren't you?"

"I don't mean to be impolite," said John, "but I know what I'm allowed to do. My parents don't mind me coming up here, so why should you, or anyone else? That's just stating a fact. If we were trespassing it would be different, but we're not. It's a public place and you have no right to tell us what to do."

The spy's hand moved to his coat pocket and John's heart jumped in his chest. He took a backward step and almost tumbled from the ledge. The man's arm shot out and grabbed him by the shirtfront, pulling him away from the drop.

"You see? It's not safe here. You must be careful."

He took his hand out of his pocket and there was a tissue in it, which he used to blow his nose. Then he suddenly turned and made his way down the slope. A few minutes later there was a scrambling sound from above, and then the boys were being confronted by uniformed police.

"Who are you? What are you doing here?" asked a Chinese sergeant.

"Not again?" groaned Peter, rolling his eyes.

John said, "We're just visiting the cave, that's all. We're going home now, all except him."

The sergeant's torch shone on the tramp.

"Ah, Yam Yam," said the policeman. "You can't stay here tonight. Best you go back to Central, eh?"

"Yes, sir. Yes, sir. Yam Yam go."

And with that the old man scrambled down the slope too, leaving the two boys to follow.

Once John and Peter reached John's flats they telephoned Jenny, using the janitor's phone in the entrance hall to the building, and were relieved to find she was home.

"Yam Yam scared me," she explained, "but once I saw who it was I told him not to be so silly. Xu's gone missing though . . ."

"We know," said John. "Yam Yam must have frightened him into leaving. It's a good job, because some of the refugees have got out and the place is swarming with police. What we've got to do early tomorrow is find Xu. Don't ask me how, but we've got to try."

"Okay, see you in the morning."

John put the phone down. Paper was being blown around the entrance hall by gusting winds that came in through the open doorway. There was a dampness to the air which was more than just high humidity.

"Not much more we can do tonight, Pete. You'd better get home."

"Yeah, okay. See you later."

John went to the lift and opened the doors, but was alarmed to see Alex standing inside, waiting for him.

"What are you doing?" John said. "Are you spying on me."

"Yep," said Alex, candidly, "and you're up to something, bruv, ain't you just? 'Course, I can keep things to myself, know what I mean Tel?" Alex touched his nose the way he had seen Arthur Daley do it, in the television series *Minder*.

"I'm not going to give you any money, Alex."

Alex raised his ten-year-old eyebrows.

"Oh, what? I should cocoa. Okay bruv, I hate keeping secrets anyway," he said, then after a short pause, he asked, "Who's this Zoo bloke you've got to find? Who's Zoo? Get it," he nudged John in the ribs. "Who's Who?"

John got into the lift and gritted his teeth. He had

no idea how much Alex knew about his activities, but he suspected his younger brother could rouse his parent's suspicions to the point where they would ask John questions point blank which he would have to answer. It was one thing to evade telling the truth, but it was quite another to tell an outright lie to his parents.

He turned to the smug face just below his.

"I'll give you five, no, *ten* dollars on pocket money day, and no haggling, or I'll take the offer back. I'm giving it to you," he added, grinding his teeth, "because you're such a good brother to me. Understand?"

"Done," said Alex.

"And you're a bloomin' crook," added John.

"Nope," said his younger brother, unashamed of his actions, "I'm a businessman. Know what I mean, Tel?"

And he touched the side of his nose again and laughed.

Chapter Ten

Once Xu was in the streets, he felt a little safer. The man who had come up to the cave had looked wild and dangerous. Xu had never seen such a fierce fellow, with his straggly black hair and beard flying in the wind, and his dirty face. Xu had yelled in alarm, when the man entered the cave, and the wild man had screamed back at him. This had frightened the Beijing youth into racing down the slope. The wild man had shouted after him, shaking his fist, and no doubt made all sorts of terrible threats and curses. The cave must have been the wild man's home, because he seemed to know exactly where it was, and had obviously climbed up to it on purpose.

The streets of Kowloon were full of people rushing here, there and everywhere. Again he noticed that unlike Beijing, there were no bicycles. Xu could not understand that. In his own city, far in the north, there were thousands and thousands of bicycles, and very few cars and trucks. Here in Hong Kong, the roads were so crammed with traffic it could hardly move, and indeed often stopped still for long periods of time while motorists honked their horns.

The pavements too, were full of people, all with anxious looks on their faces, some of them almost running. They were pouring on and off buses, and into and out of the railway stations, as if the world was going to explode any moment and they did not want to get caught outside when it did.

Watching for policemen, Xu mixed with the crowds and allowed himself to be carried on to the west, through tenements that looked about to fall down on his head, with ferns growing out of the drains, and roofs and balconies bristling with wires and aerials. He strolled by shops he had seen the last time he had been in the streets, and was stopped by a man selling watches, and had to shake his head and walk away quickly. Silk scarves, neckties, coloured handkerchiefs – it seemed they were almost being given away.

Eventually his wanderings took him into a dock-lands area, where the activity was just as frantic, even though the sun had gone down. Floodlights lit the harbour area, where boats of all shapes and sizes ploughed the waters, as numerous as the cars in the streets. Hong Kong was indeed the noisy bustling place he had heard it to be, but nothing could have prepared him for such feverish activity as he witnessed here, both on the land and on the sea.

He followed the waterfront, going south, passing stalls that sold live snakes for the pot, and crabs hissing in cauldrons of boiling water, and glass tanks full of swimming, gawping fish, large and small, that were destined to end their days on a meal table.

Over the streets, sticking out from the sides of buildings, were brightly coloured neon signs, which informed the passersby what was being sold in that particular place.

Almost every other place he passed was a restaurant of some kind, selling exotic foods. Xu could read the neon signs of course, written in Chinese characters, and noted Thai, Korean, Szechuen, Shanghai, Indian, Burmese, and many other countries, including some places he had never heard of, like MacDonalds, Burger King, and Pizza House, wherever they were. The food smelled delicious and made his stomach churn. Then he found, right there on a windowsill, a white box half-filled with fried rice and fishballs. No one seemed to want it, because they just passed it by, so he grabbed the box and wolfed down the contents, feeling ten times better afterwards.

Just as he was throwing the empty box into the gutter, and wiping his mouth on his sleeve, a face appeared above the windowsill. It was a youth about Xu's age and his eyes widened with disbelief, as they went from Xu's satisfied features, to the box in the gutter, and back again.

"Whaaaaaaa!" cried the youth, and leapt agilely through the open window.

Xu did not wait for the youth's feet to hit the pavement before taking off like a rabbit along the street. When he glanced behind him, two more boys had joined the first. They had come dashing out of a nearby butcher's shop and had obviously responded to the youth's call for assistance. Xu's stomach turned over when he noticed they were brandishing large knives. They were yelling like savages as they charged through the crowds, close on his heels. The original youth, the owner of the box of rice and fishballs, had somehow got his hands on a meat chopper, which he was waving above his head.

The sight of these maniacs flourishing weapons was enough to put the fear of death into Xu. His legs were suddenly pumping with energy and he flew along the street, weaving in and out of passersby with the skill of a slalom skier.

Then, when he rounded a corner, he saw a policeman on the far side of the road. The policeman began running, not towards Xu, but directly for the three youths following him. When the uniformed constable was halfway across the road, cars whizzing round him hooting their horns, the three boys disappeared magically down side alleys, melting into the shadows. It was as if they had never been there.

Xu dropped his run to a walk, so as not to attract the policeman's attention, and soon he was free of pursuers altogether. He felt exhilarated, as if he had just outrun the PLA tanks, and was a hero to his fellow students. He continued his walk towards the harbour.

Eventually, he reached Hong Kong harbour proper, where a clock tower stood, and some beautiful buildings, new and clean, rose out of the ground like pristine monuments to wealth. The array of lights on the far side of the water, on Hong Kong Island, was fantastic and took his breath away. With his stomach full he could afford to linger, watching blind street musicians playing a mixture of western and oriental music.

Then he entered some shopping precincts where the goods were displayed as if they were museum pieces. Very few people were buying in these sacred halls, with names like Gucci, Yves St Laurent, Lane Crawford, Marks and Spencer, and others that had not bothered to put their names in Chinese characters alongside the English. They sold leather handbags with gold clasps that might have been amongst the treasures of an ancient Mandarin. They sold silk ties covered in flowers and peacocks. They sold dresses for women rich with colour. He passed shops with shelves full of bottles of perfume, the escaping fragrances of which made his head spin.

He picked up a bottle and took the stopper out to smell it.

"Hey!" yelled a shop assistant. She was a hawk-faced lady with enough make-up on her face to last a Beijing girl for a year or more.

When she advanced towards him, he hastily replaced the stopper, but missed the counter when he went to put the bottle back in its original position. It fell to floor with a crash, followed by a shriek from the painted lady. Shards of glass went everywhere, and perfume splashed his legs.

He got out of there quickly, retreating along the marble passageways at a fast pace, though not running. He was fed up with running away from people.

It was so quiet in those halls; the people there were so sedate and smooth, he believed he had entered a holy place, a place of temples, to some elegant god.

Once outside in the streets again, Xu began to retrace his steps. He remembered that the children who were looking after him had promised to get him some papers, so that he could stay in this remarkable city of Hong Kong. He wanted to do that now. It frightened him, this noisy brightly-lit city, but he did not want to be sent back to the Chinese mainland, where he might be arrested and imprisoned – or worse.

So he made his way back to the place from which he had come, having made careful note of the street names and landmarks on his journey west and south. Xu was an intelligent youth, well used to travelling city streets on foot, and did not make the mistake of getting lost. He decided he could not go back to the cave, with the wild man occupying it, but there was a place he had been taken to, where he could hide until morning.

He was aware that the wind was rising steadily.

Chapter Eleven

When John rose at five o'clock the next morning, to sneak out of the flat, he could hear the wind and rain outside. When he had arrived back in the flat the previous evening, the television announcer had warned that a typhoon was on its way up from the Philippines, where it had created extensive damage and caused loss of life. The warning signals for an approaching typhoon, went in five stages, straight from 1 to 3 to 8 to 9 to 10. Number 10 was a hurricane and was likely to make buildings sway, blow in windows and air conditioners, and bring down landslips, telegraph poles and pylons, as well as blowing over cars and tearing the more flimsy buildings to pieces. A full typhoon was a killer. Ships would run for typhoon shelters at the hoisting of No.

3. Everyone would go home and prepare for the worst at the hoisting of No. 8.

At eleven o'clock the previous evening, Warning Signal No.1 had changed to Warning Signal No.3, which meant that strong winds gusting up to 100 kilometres per hour were being experienced in Hong Kong.

John wanted to go out and look for Xu while the streets were relatively empty, when the next signal after 3 was hoisted and people were confined to their flats. He crept out through the front door and took the lift down to the streets.

Already there were twigs being torn from the trees. If the cyclone that brought the typhoon did not veer away, those twigs would become branches, and then the trees themselves.

John hurried through the grey streets, unseasonally cool, and searched the alleys round about for signs of Xu. He did not hold out much hope, but he felt he had to try to find the youth. John only hoped the Chinese boy had the knowledge to find himself a safe place until the typhoon blew over.

By seven o'clock, John had still not found Xu, and finally decided he would have to go home. In the alley that led from the MTR to the main road, he encountered a familiar figure. It was the round-faced man with the insecty eyes.

"Where are you going?" asked the man, blocking his passage.

John was a little frightened, even though the man was no taller than himself. The man had a particularly aggressive way of talking, as if he was very sure of his ability to cause physical harm.

"Home," replied John.

"Who you look for, boy? I see you look for somebody."

"My little brother," John said. "I was sent out to fetch him."

The space containing the insects got smaller as the man narrowed his eyes.

"You lie, boy. Your brother in house."

Suddenly John became incensed. What did this man know about his home? It sounded as if the whole family was being spied on.

"What do you know about my house?" shouted John. "My father will have something to say about this! You get out of my way. I'll call for the police. Your superior will have something to say about this."

The round-faced man smiled.

"You no call for policeman. I tell policeman you look for eye-eye. I tell policeman . . ."

John suddenly noticed there was a black plastic bag full of rubbish behind the man. He stepped forward quickly and gave the man a push in the chest, sending him flying backwards. The startled Chinese man fell onto his back, his chubby arms flailing, and John heard the air whoosh out of his lungs. The rubbish bag split open and cans and bottles fell out, as well as a slimey mess which oozed between the man's fingers.

"I kill you for that!" the man wheezed, his face distorted with anger and hatred.

"You leave me alone," said John.

The man struggled amongst the rubbish, red-faced, like a beetle trying to right itself, but luckily for John he kept slipping on the cold remains of a dinner. John trotted round him and along the alley to the road. He crossed quickly and climbed the hill. He glanced behind once, but the round-faced man was nowhere to be seen.

When he got back to the flat, his mother remonstrated with him.

"Where have you been? What about school?"

"I can be ready for school in time. I went out for a walk. Anyway, there won't be any school if number eight goes up."

Alex chortled. "Early days yet, bruv."

John's father marched into the room, putting on his tie. "It's going to be a big wind," he said.

"You always say that," replied John.

Mr Tenniel nodded his head slowly. "This time I mean it. What's for breakfast boys?"

"Bake necks," said Alex.

When everyone stared at him, he explained, "That's what my Australian friend calls 'bacon and eggs'."

At three o'clock in the afternoon, the No. 8 signal was hoisted and the children were all sent home. John's dad had to stay on at work, at China Light and Power, to help with preparations for the possible No. 9 signal going up. The electricity companies needed to secure buildings and make sure all their staff knew their duties in an emergency.

Alex was already indoors helping his mother put crosses of masking tape on the windows, in case they shattered. John went on to the balcony and took in the rattan chairs and the plants. Carpets were then rolled back and all furniture secured in the middle of the rooms. Beds were moved away from the air conditioners, in case the heavy metal boxes were blown inside by the strong winds. There was a kitchen cupboard which was always kept stocked with enough provisions to last for four days, plus a calor gas cooker, candles and matches.

Finally, Dad arrived back at the flat, and they all sat down to wait out the storm.

John was terribly worried about Xu and could only pray that the youth realised what was going on and found himself somewhere to shelter from the cyclone.

The full force of the typhoon hit that night. They had watched the wobbling aircraft coming in to land at Kai Tak airport, some of them having to make second and third attempts in the high winds, until eventually the airport closed and the planes were diverted. The Philippines was the nearest airport, but the winds were still high there too, so most of the aircraft went on to Taiwan. John could imagine the passengers of some of those last landing attempts, green with fright, as the planes came down through the narrow channel of low buildings between the high risers. Even from the balcony he could see the way the aircraft were shaking and dipping, and it must have felt ten times worse for those actually inside.

Eventually too, there was a time for residents to find the innermost room in their apartments to protect themselves.

John's family all huddled in one bedroom, listening to the wind screaming round the corners of the flats. The whole building swayed violently, back and forth, making furniture travel across the floor, scraping and squealing as it did so, and gouging grooves in the parquet tiles.

Alex said, "Is the block going to snap in half?"

A kitchen window was smashed by a flying piece of rock the size of a house brick, but after Dad had investigated he came back to the bedroom. There was nothing he could do, although the wind was now opening and shutting kitchen cupboard doors, making a terrible racket. Outside, oil drums and pieces of cars were being slammed against the brickwork of the building. Telegraph poles were coming down like felled timber, and trees were shrieking as boughs were ripped away at the sockets and were hurled through the air like fletched spears.

The winds were gusting at over 200 kilometres per hour.

A television aerial that had snapped from its pole, went whizzing by the window, and then tangled itself in the drain pipe. The noise of the wind was now like the drone of a thousand bombers. Clattering objects struck the outside brickwork with discordant irregularity, as if trying to force an entry through solid concrete.

Suddenly there was a lull and everything went peaceful. The wind had completely died outside and the stillness was eerie and threatening.

"Is it over?" asked Alex. "Can I go out to play now?"

Dad said, "I think we're in the eye of the hurricane. In a few minutes the wind will be back, but it'll be swirling in the opposite direction. All that debris it's blown to one side of the colony, it'll now blow to the other."

"Put everything back in it's place," said John.

"Hardly," replied Dad.

There was a gathering clattering sound then, as the hurricane returned. This time the buffeting gusts slammed into the west side of the building, making it seem to John and Alex that a giant was charging with his shoulder, battering against the block of flats. The whole structure juddered each time a new onslaught was felt, and it indeed seemed as if the block might break in two.

"Here we go again," smiled Mum, and though John knew she was frightened, as they all were, she did not show it one bit. He thought the world of his mother in times like this.

"I hope Superman's not caught out, flying around in this," shouted Alex, as the noise grew in volume, "he'll get his hair messed up, ha, ha."

When it was all over, they discovered that a balcony glass door had shattered, in the living-room. There was glass all over the floor and much of the furniture had been damaged. Not a picture remained on the wall, and some things, like Mum's favourite porcelain vase, was not even there, having been sucked outside and taken away on the back of the wind.

"What a mess!" cried Alex in a delighted voice, wading through glass which crunched under his feet. "It'll take *weeks* for you to clean it up."

"What's all this *you* business," answered Dad. "You're helping too, you know."

Alex groaned, "But I'm only a little kid, and I'm *tired*."

"If you're so tired," said Mum, starting to pick stuff off the floor, "then go to bed."

Alex looked terrified, then bent to help his mother with the books that had been flying like birds around the room.

They all put their backs into it, with a lot of encouraging remarks from Alex, who now seemed to see it as his job to keep morale up.

When most of the work had been done, and there was some semblance of order to the flat, John tried to ring Jenny, but the telephone system was out of order. Every time he picked up the phone there was already someone on the other end, permanently connected and trying to get through herself, because each time John listened she said, "*Wai? Wai? Wai?*", the monotonous Cantonese equivalent of "*hello, who's there*", which has been known to drive some Europeans mad when they are trying to reach an English speaker.

Unable to get anywhere with the phone, John left

the flat and went out into the streets. The chaos inside his own home was multiplied a thousandfold out in the streets. Debris was everywhere, with uprooted shrubs, loose timber, iron posts, glass, branches of trees, trunks of trees, washing poles, paving stones, and all kinds of heavy and light rubbish now impeding cars and pedestrians. John picked his way over the small stuff, and climbed over broken street lamps as if they were fallen trees blocking a jungle path.

At the bottom of the hill, he paused to think.

Now where would I go, if I were Xu? he asked himself. *Where did I take him that he would run to in an emergency?*

John could not entertain the thought that Xu had been caught outside, because that would have been too terrible to contemplate. If Xu had not reached shelter he could be badly hurt, or even dead, and it would be partly John's fault for trying to help the youth in the first place.

Suddenly, it came to him.

The underground station concourse!

It was the place where any homeless people, like Yam Yam, went to when a typhoon was imminent.

John made his way to the MTR station, and on reaching there, went down the frozen escalators to the concourse below. There were indeed quite a few people down there and John scanned the faces anxiously, looking for signs of Xu. Yam Yam was there, and smiled his vacant smile at John, but no Beijing youth was in evidence.

With a sinking heart John was about to run back up

the stairs and begin searching the streets again, when he thought of something else.

He ran the length of the concourse and whipped back the curtain to the photo booth where they had taken Xu for his fake ID picture.

There, asleep on the stool, with his back against the wall of the booth, was Xu.

It seemed sensible to John to take Xu straight back up the Third Dragon and install him in the cave again. After all, the place had been visited by the police and the Chinese secret agent, and for all they knew only Yam Yam was living there. There is no more secure hiding place for someone who wants to remain under cover, than a place that has already been searched by his enemies.

So, Xu was returned to his old home, and seemed happy to see his cave once again. One of the water pipes had been damaged in the typhoon, up on the ridge that led from the high reservoir, and now Xu had a stream running past him in which he could wash. John made motions not to drink the water, for it might have been contaminated, but at least the youth could keep himself clean. Chinese people hate being in the least bit dirty, and this added convenience seemed like a lucky heaven-sent gift to Xu.

Chapter Twelve

The next few days were spent clearing the streets and getting Hong Kong back to normal. Everything had been disrupted, from the electricity supply, to the roads, to the sewage system. Everyone went out to do their bit, so that the technicians could be left free to get the services back in working order. The armed forces were called in to help.

The Gurkhas, who patrolled the border with China and had most of their camps up in the New Territories, went out into the fields to assist the Chinese farmers in salvaging what was left of their crops, duck farms, and fish lakes. The small wiry Nepalese men, who terrorised their enemies in battle with their fierce determination, removed their famous *kukri* knives and became hard but gentle workers for the Hakka farmers.

The Royal Engineers too, were in great demand, as there had been landslips and collapsed bridges and erosion under the flyovers. A hurricane brings not only high winds, but fast flowing floodwaters too, which strip away subsurface soil, leaving whatever is on top to collapse in on itself.

Members of the Dragon Troop, recruited from the Hong Kong Chinese population, went out with both the Gurkhas and the Engineers to act as interpreters.

Helicopters buzzed across the sky and bulldozers rumbled along the town and country roads.

All this activity was watched by Xu from his high vantage point. His three friends took turns in carrying food and water to him, always on the lookout for the Chinese spy. They had to be extra careful now that they knew they were being observed.

Once back at school, Jenny finally brought word that the identity card was ready for collection. Her cousin had phoned her and said that Yeung Ng was at last in a position to do business with them, but they had to go to Kowloon Walled City to take possession of the ID card. Ng refused to risk walking through the streets with an extra ID card because, since the breakout of the Vietnamese refugees, the police were stopping people and making them identify themselves. If they were not satisfied, the police were also searching people and someone with *two* ID cards would be in serious trouble.

"We've got to hold the raffle for the Swiss army knife in the morning," said Peter, "if we're going to the Walled City tomorrow evening. Tell all the kids to bring their pocket money."

So, during break, the three of them went around the playing fields whispering into ears. Inevitably McAnders noticed something was going on, and approached John.

"Whisper in my ear Tenniel," said the bigger boy.

"Pardon?" replied John, feigning ignorance.

"You heard what I said. Why are you and your wimpy friends going round buzz-buzz-buzzing? If there's something going on, I want to know about it. What's the secret?"

John sighed. He knew it would be useless trying to keep the raffle from McAnders. If John didn't explain things to him, then the older boy would corner someone who would. John decided it would sound better coming from him.

"We're just keeping it quiet because of the teachers. I didn't think you would be interested. We're raffling a Swiss army knife, tomorrow morning."

"That's illegal," said McAnders. "You could be expelled for that. That's . . ." he seemed to be searching his mind for a word ". . . that's exploitation, that is."

"Oh, come on. You've raffled things in the past. What about that old watch? It didn't even work."

Peter, on seeing McAnders confronting John, had wandered over to where they stood and was listening silently, his eyes going from one face to the other.

McAnders said, "Yeah, but that's past history,

115

Tenniel. I dunno that I can keep quiet about this. I mean, if I was to win the knife, well I might not be able to split on you, see? But otherwise, might be difficult to keep stumm."

He grinned like a shark, cold and merciles.

"I'm not fixing the raffle, McAnders, but I'm willing to cut you in. Tell you what. Anything we make over eighty dollars, you can have. How's that?"

Peter unfolded his arms and said, "Now wait a minute . . ."

John waved him quiet.

"No, we must protect the raffle. If McAnders can take care of that side of things, he deserves to be paid for it."

"Just one thing," said McAnders.

"What's that?" asked John.

"Why eighty dollars? Why not just split it with me, four ways? What's this eighty dollars touch?"

Peter intervened, a little annoyed.

"We need that amount for a special reason. We *have* to make eighty dollars. The rest we don't care about, even if it's a hundred or two hundred over. You can have whatever it is, after we take out eighty. Is it a deal?"

McAnders found his shark grin again.

"Deal," he said, and swung away from them.

Peter glared at John.

"What did we have to do that for? I hate giving that big-mouthed toad money."

John said, "You have to forget personal things in business. We had to cut him in or he would have split on us. Anyway, now we've told him he can have everything left over after we've taken our eighty dollars, he'll be encouraging people to spend their money, won't he? All his cronies will have to fork out, just to build up the kitty. See what I mean?"

Peter smiled now.

"Yeah, see what you mean."

The raffle was held the following morning with very successful results for the trio, but McAnders only came out of it with fifteen dollars, since the total take had been ninety-five dollars. What was more, he had spent five dollars of his own money, in the hope that he would win the knife. The prize was in fact won by JM, the sallow boy with the peeling nose, who was high on the teachers' hitlist for cheek. Every single day the talk in the teachers' staff room during break consisted of 5 percent leisure activities, 5 percent local gossip, and 90 percent what Jameson Master had done or said during music lessons, or maths, or English, or science, or any one of the classes he attended. Some of the teachers thought he made their lives hell, but a few enjoyed the cut and thrust of mixing with JM, and even admired his command of vocabulary and the inventiveness of his remarks.

"I won," yelled JM, "I got the knife. Look, it's even got one of those spike things for taking stones out of horse's hooves."

"Quiet!" hissed Peter. "Keep it down."

When Slimeball passed their desk, JM asked the teacher innocently, "Got any stones in your left hoof you want taken out?"

117

"WHAT?" cried Mr Ball, who had recently begun dealing with JM by feigning anger at every word the boy spoke. "HOW DARE YOU! What do you mean by suggesting such a thing? My left *hoof*?" Mr Ball had always told his wife that a teacher needed to be a good actor if he was to discipline his class properly, so even when he was feeling calm, he blew his top in fury. Mr Ball was of the opinion that if you ranted and raved about some small infringment of the rules, students would wonder what they would get for doing something *really* bad.

"I'm sorry," said JM, who was immune to anger, false or otherwise, "what about the other hoof then?"

Mr Ball was about to destroy JM with baleful breath when his eyes alighted on the Swiss army knife JM was fingering.

"I'll confiscate that, if you don't mind," said Slimeball, and whipped it out of JM's hand before he knew from which direction the wind was blowing.

Thus in the course of five minutes, JM had owned and lost a beautiful Swiss army knife.

In the afternoon, John was approached by McAnders.

"Fifteen dollars is paltry," said the youth.

"It's all right for nothing," replied John. "I told you we needed eighty for something special, otherwise we wouldn't have raffled the knife."

"I still think you could have split the money four ways. I got a lot of people interested in that raffle. Put in a bit of legwork over that. You might not have

118

made even eighty without me." That much was probably true.

"Well, I'm sorry, McAnders. We're not splitting this money between ourselves. It's for a friend who needs it badly, one of the local Chinese. He'll be . . . evicted from his home if he doesn't get eighty dollars."

"Do-gooders, eh? Dudley Do-rights."

"If you want to put it that way, yes," replied John. "We were asked to help, even before the typhoon struck, so we're keeping our promise. Sorry."

McAnders shrugged.

"In a good cause, I suppose – but if I find you lot using that money for yourselves, I'm going to get my cut, even if I have to wring it out of you, understand?"

"Fair enough."

Later, John and Jenny went up the Third Dragon to see Xu.

"We're getting you an identity card today," said John, and Jenny wrote the characters down on a piece of paper. Xu nodded enthusiastically. "You'll soon be able to go down into Hong Kong. Maybe you can find a community of Mandarin speakers, until you learn Cantonese? There must be some around . . ."

When they left him, Xu seemed to have cheered up considerably. Jenny said he had been feeling terribly homesick, and kept thinking of his mother and father.

"He wants to get a message to them, to let them know he's all right," she said, "so I'm going to write to this address he's given me. I only hope the letter's not intercepted by the Chinese authorities. Xu's parents will be sick with worry."

"Well, let's get this ID card, then Xu can write to them himself."

John agreed to meet Jenny outside the Walled City at five o'clock and they would go in together and find Jenny's cousin. He, in turn, would lead them to Yeung Ng. Peter could not be with them because his father had asked him to take some visitors to Tiger Balm Gardens. Peter had promised to call them later, when they returned.

Unknown to all three of the teenagers, a man had been watching John and Jenny climb up the Third Dragon to the cave, and saw them come down again. When they had gone their different ways, he too took the path up the hill. As he came to the cave, he paused, extracted a handkerchief from his pocket and wiped his sweaty hands and face with it, then carefully drew out a revolver. Taking a firm grip of the weapon, he advanced towards the place where Xu was sitting, quietly humming to himself.

John approached the slumland called the Walled City at exactly five minutes to five. In his pocket was two-hundred-and-forty dollars. It was a bustling time in the streets, with people coming home from work. The hawker stalls were busy and the smells of their various cooking foods filled the warm evening air. There was a Tin Hau, or fisherman's temple, attached to the giant slum, and people were burning incense, adding to the mixed odours in the street. Red and gold decorations, the lucky colours, glittered in the evening sun.

At the side where he was standing, the slum city was about twelve to fourteen storeys high and stretched three hundred yards along the street: a solid mass of ramshackle dwellings fitting into each other as awkwardly as misshapen boxes. The whole structure looked as if it would topple in a strong wind, yet it had survived several typhoons, though not without damage. That was because it was as deep as it was long: five thousand shanties locked together in a single block. Imagine a derelict football stadium that had been filled up with shacks and piled up to a height of a hundred feet. Think of how dank and dark it would be in the middle. Think of the maze of tunnels you would need to get to each individual shack. That describes the Walled City, which had once belonged to the Manchus when it was an island fortress in the middle of a British colony.

Hanging from the outside of dingy shops were flattened ducks, suckling pigs and bunches of tiny quails. Displayed in baskets were aged black eggs, chicken's feet, fish lips, and all the foodstuffs which European *gwailos* find so unsavoury. The black eggs were said to be a hundred years old, but John knew that was untrue, though they were, for eggs, quiet ancient. They had been injected with huge amounts of salt to preserve them.

Amongst the vegetables and fruit were durians,

which looked like big green pineapples, smelled like rotting silage, but tasted as sweet as honey. When you ate one you had to hold your nose. Also there was basket on basket of *choi sum*, the favourite vegetable of the Chinese people, which looked like and had some of the properties of spinach.

John stood outside the Tin Hau temple, where he had promised to meet Jenny. He searched the bustling street with his eyes. While walking to the Walled City he had had the distinct feeling that he was being followed. Once, when he had turned around quickly, he thought he saw someone duck into a doorway, but he couldn't be sure.

As John stared into the black alleys that peppered the side of the Walled City, he was approached by a thin man in a string vest, khaki shorts and straw hat.

"What you want, boy?" asked the Chinese man in English. "Why you look here. You want see *poor* people?"

The man obviously thought John had come to gloat over the poverty that was inherent in the Walled City. John shook his head vigorously and said in Cantonese, "I'm no *gwailo*. I'm part Chinese. I have friends who live inside."

The grizzled face retreated a little.

"Oh, you're Canton man?"

"My mother is Cantonese."

The man's attitude changed in an instant. "You want to buy something? You want to buy a copy watch?"

Copy watches were fake Rolexes and Cartiers, sold

on the street. The vendors showed you a photograph of lots of watches and you chose one you liked. A runner would be dispatched to a nearby flat and the watch would be in your hands within minutes.

"No," said John, "I don't want a copy watch. I don't want anything. I haven't got any money."

"Oh."

The man lost interest and faded into a shop doorway with the word NOODLE written over the door. That meant you could buy noodles there – a hundred different varieties – but the Chinese do not like plurals. At the station the signs said TO PLATFORM, even though there were five plat-forms, and outside camera shops were notices like MANY CAMERA FOR SALE. It was the same in their own language. There are no plurals in Cantonese.

John waited until nearly half-past-five and still no Jenny appeared. In the end he decided he would have to go inside the Walled City alone, and ask around until he found Jenny's cousin, or Yeung Ng.

He entered an alley which was nothing more than a black hole in the side of the slum.

Once he had gone inside, a figure stepped out of the shadows of the noodle shop, and followed behind him.

Chapter Thirteen

Once inside the narrow crooked passage, John tried to keep a sense of direction, and noted some objects to assist his journey out of the maze. However, the tunnels were not even on one level, dipping and rising, twisting and turning, and all the time growing darker, until he could hardly see his own feet.

Everywhere was damp and slippery. There was a constant flow of water down the walls and John was horrified to see loose electricity cables following the tunnels, hanging in careless bunches from the low ceilings, covered in filth and huge spiders' webs. When he looked up, he could see small grey shapes running along the cable pathways, into holes in the upper reaches, where the ceilings occasionally disappeared into blackness. Rats! They were on the slick concrete floor too, running over cobbles and slipping away into corners.

The further he went into the interior, the more he came across dwellings that opened directly onto the passageways.

Inside these places, dimly-lit by 15-watt unshaded bulbs, were large families clustered in the gloom. They did not seem to be doing very much except sitting on rusting bedframes, or on chairs around a table that was covered with an oilcloth. Some were playing mah jong, but others were simply staring into space.

Then there were rooms with wire coffins only large enough for a man to sleep inside. Here lived the "cage people", who locked themselves in their small chicken coops for security when they went to sleep. During their waking hours they rapped and clattered mah jong tiles around rickety tables. Mah jong, or "chattering sparrows", so called because of the sound of the tiles clicking together, was their only reason for living. They played it continually, fingering symbols for four winds they never felt on their cheeks any more; for dragons that flew through spring and autumn skies that were denied them in their dim cells; for bamboo and flowers they had not smelled or touched in many a long dark year.

They were like shadows, or ghosts, these old men: waiting for something that was never going to come. Waiting for eternity to end. Waiting for the city to split apart and let the sunlight reach their grey skins, their pale eyes. They did not inhabit their mean little rooms, they haunted them. The fungus grew on the walls around them, the air was fetid and stifling, the smells were those of rotting plaster and wood. Everywhere was damp in this sunless underworld.

Outside the rooms, there was rubbish in the passageways where the rats feasted. There were cockroaches clustered in their thousands: cockroaches the size of a man's nose, oily-black and glistening in the poor light, their ridged yellow undersides showing when they tumbled from the shifting heaps of garbage, and fell on their backs.

Several times John came to crossroads, or dead ends, so that he had to change direction, taking a left or right fork, or up some rickety stairs to another uneven set of passageways. This was indeed a subterranean netherworld of shadow people. He passed recesses in the wall where old women were shelved, laying asleep as if they were already entombed in the stone vaults they would inhabit after death.

There were one or two objects covered in rust and dust, rags and litter, which he had to jump over. One of these was an old cannon barrel and John wondered how long it had been lying there. Perhaps since the Manchus had ruled China?

When he came to an air shaft, he looked up, through the dangling cables and ugly projections, to see daylight. Though it was a grey light, filtered by clouds of dust and having to navigate angles and corners which impeded its progress, it was at least an indication that there was an outside world. A kitten nestled on a nearby ledge, staring down at him curiously.

There were footsteps behind him and John suddenly became aware that he was being followed. Kowloon Walled City is the birthplace and central home of the notorious Chinese gangs known as the Triads. They ruled the bowels of the giant slum, collecting protection money from shopkeepers, terrorising decent people, and robbing anyone foolish enough to enter the alleys of the lawless city alone. The police were trying to stamp them out, of course, but they were like cockroaches. They were difficult to find, they scattered when the law approached them, and they hid in cracks in the walls where no one could find them.

The footsteps behind John were tentative, as if someone was searching for someone, and he quickened his pace. He knew that he was lost now and had to ask the way. He stopped by an old man, lying in a recess in the wall.

"Do you know Yeung Ng?" he asked the old man in Cantonese. "Can you tell me the way to where Yeung Ng lives?"

The old man, thin and wizened from smoking opium, shook his head sadly.

John hurried on, coming across a neatly-dressed schoolboy on his way to the outside.

"Hello, can you tell me where Yeung Ng lives?"

The schoolboy looked at John with wide eyes.

"Yeung Ng? He lives seven streets away . . ."

Just then, a youth stepped out of the deeper

shadows, from behind an iron grill.

The schoolboy hurried on his way.

The youth, lean and quick as a cobra, leapt in front of John.

"You are asking about Yeung Ng?" said the boy.

"Yes," replied John.

"*Nei yau gei doh chin-aa?*" snapped the youth, asking how much money John had with him.

"Any money I have is for Ng," replied John. "If you take me to him, perhaps he will pay you?"

"Perhaps I will stab you," shouted the youth, "unless you give me your money?" His hand went to his pocket.

Just at that moment the person who had been following John appeared by his side. The newcomer spoke.

"Having trouble with this one?"

John was astonished and not a little relieved to see that it was McAnders.

McAnders was a head taller than the Chinese youth, who now looked a little concerned. The youth drew a knife from his pocket, slowly, and backed against the wall. McAnders reached down and picked up a loose brick lying amongst others by the wall.

"I wouldn't try to use that knife, if I were you, fella," he said in his broad Australian accent. "People have been known to get hurt that way."

The Chinese youth swore and melted into the alley wall.

John almost collapsed with relief.

"Thanks McAnders. You saved my bacon. What

are you doing here anyway?"

McAnders tossed the brick away, and it clumped down the alley.

"Following you, what else? What are you up to anyway?"

Seeing there was nothing else for it, John explained the whole business to McAnders, who nodded and grunted at appropriate intervals, but did not interrupt until the explanation was complete.

"So there you have it," said John.

"Why didn't you wimps tell me this before?" said the Australian boy. "I could've helped you. I know this place like the back of my hand. My father works for the Urban Council. He's responsible for re-housing the families in here – into the new flats being built at the back of Kowloon. This dump's coming down soon . . ."

"At the moment I just want to find Yeung Ng, so I can get the false ID card. Then Xu can leave the Third Dragon and make his way to Singapore or Taiwan – somewhere he will really be safe."

McAnders shook his head.

"You must be crazy coming in here without even an address. Look, I can find my way in and out, but finding a *person* in this rabbit warren is impossible. You know how many nooks and crannies there are in the Walled City? You could hide an army in here. Even with some sort of address, you would get nowhere. Do you see any door numbers? How many street names have you passed?"

"One or two . . ."

"One or two – but there are thousands of passages in here, on a dozen different levels, some of them no bigger than rabbit holes. This is the crazy house at the fun fair, man. You've got an impossible task."

"Oh," said John, bitterly disappointed.

"Come on mate," said McAnders, "let's get back outside, then we can send in a runner for him, someone who knows *all* the wormholes in this chunk of cheese. Any one of the hawker stall boys will do it for a few bucks."

"I didn't think of that," said John, mentally kicking himself. "I needn't have come in here in the first place. Okay then. Let's go."

The bigger boy led the way, back down the dingy passages, passing through areas of near-complete darkness from time to time. He pointed things out as they went.

"That's a well over there," he remarked, as they passed a deep hole with a small wall around it. "They keep a fish down there, to warn people if it's getting polluted."

"How does the fish do that?" asked John, innocently.

"It dies," came the blunt reply.

When they were three-quarters of the way back to the outside streets, they were ambushed coming round a bend. McAnders was grabbed by at least four pairs of hands and forced to the floor. John found himself in the grip of three men who held him against a wall.

McAnders struggled, yelling at his captors, but

John remained still. He could see there were too many of them. In the dim light he could also see they had a tattoo on their bare right forearms. It was an elaborate figure 4, embellished with curlicues and flourishes, drawn inside the shape of a skull. Tattooes like this denoted that the wearer was a member of a triad gang, in this case the *Sei Mong Tau*.

This particular figure is an unlucky number to the Cantonese because the word 'four' (or *sei*) is the same as the word for "death". This was obviously the *Death Head Triad*.

"Don't fight," spat a youth into the face of McAnders, and he brandished a knife in front of the Australian boy's eyes. John recognised the youth as the one that had confronted him earlier, the boy that McAnders had sent packing. "Don't fight, or I cut you bad."

"I'll ram that down your gullet," panted McAnders, but he ceased struggling. One of the triad members had his foot on the Australian boy's throat and pressed down whenever he tried to move.

John looked up as another man stepped out of a doorway, picking his teeth with a matchstick. He recognised him instantly, having met the man in the Nine Dragons Garden at Wong Tai Sin Temple.

It was Yeung Ng.

"Over here," cried John. "Mr Ng! You remember me? I've come with the money for the ID card. Tell these people we have business together."

Ng grinned and the other men laughed. He strolled over to where they were huddled and said something in a voice too low for John to hear properly and understand. Again there was laughter. It seemed there was a big joke, which was not to be shared with the *gwailos*.

John wondered what was the matter with them. He looked at McAnders.

McAnders said sourly, "Haven't you twigged yet? That bloke's with them. He's probably their leader."

Of course! John's heart sank. They would take the money now and there would be no false identity card. It was all a trick to get them inside the Walled City, played carefully and patiently. Perhaps Jenny's cousin was in on it too, though John doubted it. He had probably acted in good faith, asking around for a good forger, and this gang had seen the opportunity to make some money.

Ng said, "Give me the cash."

"No," snapped John, but the next moment, hands went through his pockets and came out with the money. McAnders, to his Australian fury, was also searched and robbed of the fifteen dollars he had been paid for keeping quiet about the raffle.

"I thought I was a rogue," said McAnders, "till I met these blokes. They make Ned Kelly look like Albert Schweitzer."

The two boys were then dragged into a sleazy room on one side of the alley. McAnders said that it was probably one vacated by people who had been rehoused. The gang tied McAnders' wrists to an iron bedstead. Then they all crowded around John, forcing him up against the wall.

"Now," said Ng, "you tell us where the Beijing student is hiding."

"What do you want to know for?" asked John.

"None of your business," snapped Ng. "You tell us or we break some fingers."

They took hold of John's hand.

"What's happening?" cried McAnders, obviously not understanding the Cantonese conversation.

John said, "They're going to hurt me because I won't tell them where Xu is. I know what they're going to do. They think I'm *selling* the ID to Xu and they want to get to him and rob him. I'm sure that's what they're planning."

"And probably murder him too," said McAnders.

Ng turned to McAnders.

"I unnerstan what you say. You tell me where is Beijing student or I break him hand!" he yelled into McAnders' face.

"Don't tell him," gasped John, the pain washing over him as they applied pressure to his fingers.

McAnders stared at John and then said, "He's up on the Third Dragon. There's a cave up on the hillside. You'll find him there."

"You sure?" snapped Ng.

"No, but that's what this bloke told me before you lot crawled out of the sewer."

Ng rapped McAnders hard on the chest.

"You lie, you *die*. You unnerstan me?"

"Perfectly," growled McAnders, "but I'm not lying."

In Cantonese Yeung Ng said, "Tie these two up.

133

We'll go to the Third Dragon and see if they're telling the truth. If the Beijing student is not there . . ." His voice trailed off.

The two boys were lashed to the iron bedstead with the nylon straps with which building labourers used to lash their bamboo scaffolding together. It was done expertly and the bonds were unbreakable. The thin straps were made to keep a network of bamboo poles together, with men crawling all over them, hanging from them, at thirty and forty storeys high. They would certainly hold two schoolboys in place for as long as the world continued to turn.

The triad gang then left the room.

"Why did you tell them?" said John. "You know what they're going to do."

"I had to, you dope. What would I say to your parents if I took you home with a broken hand? That I let some men torture you because a Chinese youth might get robbed? I *had* to tell them. I'm older then you. I'll be held responsible, not you."

That much was true and John realised he should be grateful to the other boy, but he was now desperately worried about Xu.

"We've got to get out of here," he said. "Quick, help me drag the bedstead to the door. I'll see if I can get it open and yell for help."

The two boys heaved and scraped the ironwork over to the door, but it was shut firmly. No amount of kicking did any good. They began yelling and screaming, but the likelihood was that anyone who heard would ignore the sound. This was Kowloon

Walled City and like New York or London, you minded your own business, because if you got involved in something you could end up losing more than material possessions.

However, they had not been shouting for more than five minutes – though that's a long time when you are tied to a bedstead – when the door was forced open from the other side. A frightened-looking Chinese boy confronted them.

"You John Tenniel?" said the youth.

"Yes," replied John.

"I Jenny's cousin. I see triad get you, but I no have friend to he'p me." He changed to Cantonese as he cut the boys loose with a sharp penknife. "Jenny called me on the telephone and said to look out for you. I asked around and people said they had seen you walking inside here and an old man pointed to which passage you took. When I caught up to you the triad had got you. I had to wait until they left."

"Good thanks," said John, rubbing his wrists once he was free. "Now we've got to get to Xu, before that bunch of baboons do. Are you coming McAnders?"

The Australian boy, also having been freed, gritted his teeth.

"Let's go," he said.

Chapter Fourteen

Once they were safely outside the Walled City, the two youths caught a light bus to their own area. McAnders suggested that they call the police and let the law take care of the triad gang, but despite the danger John was still worried about Xu being sent back to China. He reasoned with himself that Xu had undergone innumerable dangers in order to reach Hong Kong. Through Jenny, who exchanged written characters with Xu, he had learned that even the presence of sharks, and the loss of a companion, had not deterred the Beijing youth. If Xu had been willing to risk death to reach Hong Kong, what right had John to call in the police to protect him, because if he did so, Xu would certainly be arrested?

He explained all this to McAnders.

"You see what I mean?" said John. "I know the triad gang might beat him up, and we've got to try to prevent that, but if we call in the police, he might be sent back to China and thrown in prison or worse."

McAnders shrugged. "It's up to you. Some of the kids are playing basketball in one of the parks. Bailey and Rodin – Wanita Lau and some of the girls. Whaddya say we go and get them, on the way to the Third Dragon, and see if we can't catch up with the triad?"

John looked at McAnders with admiration.

"That's a *great* idea."

When the light bus was passing O Jau Yan Road, McAnders yelled, "*Yau lok*," meaning "someone wants to get off". The driver pulled up close to the curb and opened the doors for them.

They left the light bus and raced through the streets to the small park in O Jau Yan Road, where they saw about twelve youths racing around with a basketball. There was a lot of shouting and bumping going on amongst the players, and they didn't notice John and his companion approaching. McAnders went up to the wire fence surrounding the play area.

"Rodin! Bailey! Tam!" he yelled.

"Hey," cried a Chinese boy, David Tam, "it's Mac. C'mon Mac, we need you on our team."

"No, we've got a job on. I can't explain now, but a triad gang has gone after one of Tenniel's mates. We've got to go and help."

The boys and girls, a mixture of Australian, British, Chinese and Indian, clustered around the fence like monkeys. One or two of them looked worried.

"A *triad* gang? I mean, that's heavy tribal stuff, Mac. I dunno about this," said Khan, a tall Indian boy.

A stocky girl named Maggie Chan nodded vigorously.

"You shouldn't get mixed up with the triads."

John injected some drama into the situation.

"It's a matter of life and death," he said. "We're the only ones who can save him. If we don't go and help, nobody will."

"What about the cops?" asked Bailey.

"Can't use 'em," said McAnders. "I can't explain now. Look, are any of you lot coming, or do I have to go and sort them out on my own? What are you anyway, a bunch of wimps?"

An Australian boy called Henderson began climbing the fence rather than go all the way around the park to the gate on the other side.

"We're coming," he said, "don't lose the lolly."

Once Henderson had begun climbing the fence, Tam, Khan, Chan and Bailey followed, and finally the rest of them. They clambered up the chainlink fencing like monkeys, and dropped down to the other side.

When everyone was on the pavement, they tightened the laces of their Reeboks, it being the trend to wear them loose with the tongues flopping out. Then a tall willowy girl called Baxter shouted excitedly, "What are we waiting for? Let's go!"

John led the way, taking the pack through the streets at racing speed. He felt exhilarated. In the back of his mind was the thought that he was doing something foolish, something which he might later regret, but that thought had been pushed down and almost buried. He was caught up in the excitement of his own actions. There was no stopping the beast he had released now. Even if he himself dropped out, he knew the other older boys would go on. They had been raised to a pitch of excitement too: he could see it in their shining faces, and the way they raced along.

They reached the Lung Cheung Road and surged across, scrambling after John up the hill.

When they finally approached the cave, all was still, and John sensed it was empty. He rushed inside, crying, "Xu? Are you there? Where are you?" with no response. The cave was indeed empty. There were a few plastic water bottles lying on the ground, and some chicken bones which the ants had found, but that was all. John went to the entrance and looked out over the vast cityscape of Kowloon, which hummed and whirred, carrying on its daily business as if there was no crisis going on at the cave on the Third Dragon.

Bitterly disappointed and upset, he turned and said to McAnders, who was right behind him, "Looks like we're too late. They've got him already. We'd better discuss what to do next."

McAnders preferred action to words.

"Search the area," he yelled to his cronies.

Tam cried, "What are we looking for?"

"People, dope. There was a Chinese student

escaped from the Beijing massacre, living in this cave. Tenniel was feeding him. Now the triad gang has got him. Maybe they're still around . . ."

The youths began searching the scrubland, looking in the crevices of the hill, and even under the bushes. After half-an-hour it became obvious that there was no one on the Third Dragon but the youngsters themselves.

"What do we do, Tenniel?" asked McAnders.

"I'd better go home," said John, the guilty feelings beginning to seep through from the bottom of his conscious. "I'll tell my dad what's happened, and hope he can sort something out. I suppose I should've done that in the first place, before things got out of hand. Thanks anyway, McAnders."

The Australian boy stuck his hand out.

"Mac, to you mate."

John shook it and smiled grimly.

Then he left the teenagers who were already larking about in the cave, some of them making ghost noises, and others trying to climb down through the small hole at the back. John knew they would be there for hours now, inventing games, being kids. He climbed down the slope of the Third Dragon with a heavy heart.

When he reached the door of his flat, he breathed deeply. He knew his father was going to be upset by what he would tell him and John was not sure he would approve of his son's actions. Still, the story had to be told, and it had to be told *now*.

He put the key in the lock and turned.

The door swung open and John walked into a living-room full of people.

The first person he noticed was Xu.

John stepped forward, saying, "Xu. You're okay . . ."

He cut his sentence short, because he had recognised the man sitting next to Xu on the sofa. It was the Chinese agent, the spy, and he was sipping a cup of tea. Sitting on the right of him was Peter, and on another chair, Jenny. They both looked red-faced and anxious.

John's mother was on her feet.

"Where have you *been*? Jenny said you'd gone to the Walled City."

"I did, I mean I was there, but I got attacked by a triad gang. Then I thought they'd gone after Xu, so McAnders and his cronies came with me to stop them from hurting Xu, and then . . . then I came back here."

John couldn't take his eyes from the Chinese spy, who seemed to be enjoying the hospitality of the Tenniel home, without reservation.

John's father said, "Well, he's home now, dear. Let's get to the bottom of this mess. John, I can see you staring and it's impolite. Let me introduce you to the gentleman that seems to fascinate you so much. I gather you've met, but I'm sure you have no idea who he really is . . . this is Detective Inspector Yip."

"Inspector Yip?" said John, slowly. "You're . . ."

". . . a simple Hong Kong policeman, unfortunately," smiled the man in question, "not an exotic *spy* or secret agent. Yes thank you Mrs Tenniel, another piece of thousand-layer cake would be nice."

He took the proffered pastry in his free hand, balancing his cup and saucer in the other.

"If you're a plain-clothes policeman," said John, "who's the round-faced man with the notebook? Is he one of your men?"

"Describe him," said Inspector Yip.

John did so, and by the end of his speech the policeman was nodding his head sagely.

"You thought *I* was the spy. The man you have described has been under police observation for some time now. We believe he is a freelance agent, collecting information on local people so that he can denounce them to the Chinese authorities when Hong Kong is handed over. He's attempting to feather his nest in advance, but we'll deal with him. I think it's time we picked him up and had a word with him. You won't have any more trouble from that quarter."

Inspector Yip then addressed John again.

"Now, I have to say that it's a pity you didn't tell me what was going on that first night I bumped into you. We had reports of a student entering Hong Kong, from the underground in China. Luckily there's no real harm done. Xu here will be seen by someone from the government . . ."

"And sent back, I suppose," said John bitterly.

"As I've explained to your two friends here, that's

very unlikely, so long as we can keep his presence in Hong Kong at a low key. The less media coverage we get, the better it will be all round. We don't want to cause a deep rift with China over this – we've already incurred their displeasure over a table tennis player who remained here after the massacre – but Xu's no celebrity, so we'll probably get him away quietly. The press are really only interested in someone news-worthy, like a famous sportsman, or preferable to that, an artist or poet, or a leader of the protests. We know the authorities up there are executing many of the dissident students. No one wants to send young Xu here, back to that sort of situation."

Inspector Yip said something to Xu, who smiled and replied.

"You speak Mandarin?" said John, surprised.

"Oh yes," replied Inspector Yip, "and I have to pass on to you this young man's thanks. He said you saved his life and he will always be in your debt. He wishes you and your family longevity and hopes that one day he will be able to repay all three of you."

John said, "Tell him we appreciate that."

Jenny nodded vigorously, but Peter said, "I'll settle for not getting blasted when I get home . . ."

John's mother said, "I'll call your parents, and your's too, Jenny. I think they ought to know, but I'm sure they'll understand that you were acting in the best faith . . ."

"If a little foolishly," added Mr Tenniel.

"Thanks," replied Peter.

"Thank you, Mrs Tenniel," said Jenny.

There was a knock at the front door and John's father opened it to reveal two uniformed policemen. Inspector Yip put down his empty cup and stood up.

"My car's here," he said. "We'll get Xu to a safe place tonight and keep you informed of events. Please, do not discuss this with anyone else. I shall want the names and addresses of your other friends – who was it, McAnders? Could you give them to my sergeant please? We'll need to have a quiet word with them all. The need for secrecy is paramount."

John suddenly let out a sound of despair.

"What about the triad gang?" he cried.

Inspector Yip smiled.

"Oh, didn't I tell you? We arrested them up at the cave. They arrived just as we were collecting young Xu here. Ng, their leader, is wanted in connection with a jewellery shop robbery in Yau Ma Tei, and in any case they were all armed with knives and iron bars. They tried to deny doing anything unlawful, of course, but carrying weapons is a chargeable offence. We shall have them to ourselves for a while yet . . . long enough to be able to get Xu somewhere safe, to another country which isn't in such a sensitive position as Hong Kong."

With that, the inspector left, and Xu followed after shaking hands gravely, first with Peter, then with Jenny, and lastly with John. He looked sad to be leaving them, but John knew that at last he would be in good hands.

Xu spoke some last words, but what they were John did not know, because the inspector was out in the hall. He hoped Xu was saying that they would meet again, some day, in another place. Then Xu was urged to leave by the policeman, while the sergeant stayed to take the names and addresses of the others who had helped them.

Once the sergeant too, had left, John received a rocket from his father and mother. They told him they understood his motives, but those motives were slightly off course.

"You should have told us," Mr Tenniel said to all three youngsters. "You should have trusted us."

Peter replied, "But if we had, what would you have done? You would have told the police."

"Of course," said Mr Tenniel, "but as you can see, that was the right thing to do. Xu is being taken care of."

Peter caught John's look, and they both turned to stare at Jenny.

"What?" Mr Tenniel, looking from one to the other of them. "Why are you looking at each other like that? Is it something I said?"

Jenny took a deep breath.

"Yes, Mr Tenniel. You see, you're talking about things that have already happened, and saying that they were *bound* to happen. That's not quite true. You would have informed the police, but we didn't know *then* that Xu would not be sent back. We know it now, but we didn't know it then, do you see?

"What I'm trying to say is, we still think we did the

145

right thing. You're an adult – you've got to do what other adults would do."

"You're saying we follow rigid rules. I suppose that's true. I can't see any responsible adult taking food and water to a political refugee hidden in a cave."

"Yet Xu might have been sent back to China. No one really knew what was going to happen, until a few minutes ago, did they?" said Jenny.

Mr Tenniel grunted.

"Well, I . . ."

Mrs Tenniel interrupted.

"What Jenny's saying is correct. Grown-ups have no alternative but to do what is expected of them by other adults. They like to think they are making a choice, but in fact they have no power over their decisions. Once a person becomes an adult, society takes away their individual choice. Young people have the freedom to make decisions. We have not. It's been made for us, by the rest of the adult world. It's been taken out of our hands. Isn't that what you were saying Jenny?"

The three youngsters nodded.

"Something like that," said John.

Mr Tenniel looked at his wife as if seeing her for the first time and there was an admiration in that glance that John did not recall seeing before. John and always known his mother had a keen insight into the minds of others, whereas his dad believed everyone thought like Mr Tenniel, and those who didn't were usually wrong. It seemed like his dad had now accepted her superiority in such matters.

"Well," said Mr Tenniel, "be that as it may, *I'm* hungry. Anyone fancy a meal in Mong Kok? My treat."

Alex suddenly appeared from the depths of the flat.

"Somebody mention food? I could eat a giant jellyfish, ha, ha."

"We'll hold you to that, young man," replied Mr Tenniel, "they happen to serve pickled jellyfish at the Japanese restaurant I have in mind."

Alex looked so panic stricken they all burst out laughing.

"Come on, bruv," John said, putting an arm around Alex's drooping shoulders, "I'll help you with it. I'll hold the plate to stop it wobbling over the edge."

"Yuk!" said Alex. "I'll settle for beans on toast, instead."

MYSTERY THRILLER

Introducing, a new series of hard hitting, action packed thrillers for young adults.

THE SONG OF THE DEAD by Anthony Masters
For the first time in years 'the song of the dead' is heard around the mud flats of Whitstable. But this time is it really the ghostly cries of dead sailors? Or is it something far more sinister? Barney Hampton is sure that something strange is going on – and he's determined to get to the bottom of the mystery . . .

THE FERRYMAN'S SON by Ian Strachan
Rob is convinced that Drewe and Miles are up to no good. Why else would two sleek city whizz-kids want to spend the summer yachting around a sleepy Devonshire village? Where do they go on their frequent night cruises? And why does the lovely Kimberley go with them? Then Kimberley disappears, and Rob finds himself embroiled in a web of deadly intrigue . . .

Further titles to look out for in the Mystery Thriller series:

Treasure of Grey Manor by Terry Deary
The Foggiest by Dave Belbin
Blue Murder by Jay Kelso
Dead Man's Secret by Linda Allen

HIPPO CHEERLEADERS

Have you met the girls and boys from Tarenton High?
Follow the lives and loves of the six who form the school
Cheerleading team.

CHEERLEADERS NO 22:		
RIVALS	Ann E Steinke	£1.50
CHEERLEADERS NO 23:		
PROVING IT	Diane Hoh	£1.50
CHEERLEADERS NO 24:		
GOING STRONG	Carol Ellis	£1.50
CHEERLEADERS NO 25:		
STEALING SECRETS	Anne E Steinke	£1.50

You'll find these and many more fun Hippo books at your local bookseller, or you can order them direct. Just send off to *Customer Services, Hippo Books, Westfield Road, Southam, Leamington Spa, Warwickshire CV33 0JH*, not forgetting to enclose a cheque of postal order for the price of the book(s) plus 30p for postage and packing.

STREAMERS

We've got lots of great books for younger readers in Hippo's STREAMERS series:

Broomstick Services by Ann Jungman   £1.75
When Joe, Lucy and Jackie find two witches sleeping in the school caretaker's shed, they can't believe their eyes. When they hear that the witches want to be ordinary, they can't believe their ears. But they help the witches set up *Broomstick Services* and then the fun really begins . . .

Paws – A Panda Full of Surprises
by Joan Stimson   £1.75
Every year Uncle Cyril sends Trevor an exciting birthday present. But this year he seems to have forgotten. That is until a smart delivery truck arrives outside Trevor's house bringing the most fantastic present Trevor could ever have dreamed of – Paws!

Aristotle Sludge by Margaret Leroy   £1.75
Class 1C's routing changes completely when Aristotle Sludge explodes into their lives. Looking after a baby dinosaur means a lot of hard work – but with Aristotle Sludge around there's a lot of fun too!

The Old Woman Who Lived In A Roundabout
by Ruth Silvestre   £1.75
When Joe discovers a roundabout whilst out exploring,
he can hardly believe his eyes. And when he finds out
that an old woman lives in it, he is truly amazed. But,
before long Joe and Granny Peg become firm friends and
magical things begin to happen . . .

PRESS GANG

Why not pick up one of the PRESS GANG books, and follow the adventures of the teenagers who work on the *Junior Gazette*? Based on the original TV series produced for Central Television.

Book 1: First Edition
As editor of the brand new *Junior Gazette*, and with five days to get the first edition on the street, the last thing Lynda needs is more problems. Then an American called Spike strolls into her newsroom and announces he's been made a member of the *Gazette* team too . . .

Book 2: Public Exposure
Lynda is delighted when the *Junior Gazette* wins a computer in a writing competition. But she can't help feeling that it was all a little too easy . . . Then articles for the *Gazette* start to appear mysteriously on the computer screen. Who is the mystery writer, and why won't he reveal his identity?

Book 3: Checkmate
It's midnight, and Lynda's got to put together a whole new edition of the *Junior Gazette* by morning. The only way she can do it is to lock the office, keeping her staff in and their parents out! Spike's supposed to be taking a glamorous new date to a party – how is he going to react to being locked in the newsroom for the night?

Book 4: The Date
It's going to be a big evening for Lynda – a cocktail party where she'll be introduced to lots of big names in the newspaper business. There's only one problem: who's going to be her date? The answer's obvious to most of the *Junior Gazette* team, but Lynda is determined that the last person she'll take to the party is Spike Thomson!